Katharine's brother Darin had disappeared, somewhere in Queensland, and she could not rest until she had gone up there to see if she could find him. But the problem of Darin's whereabouts paled into insignificance in the face of the much greater problem of how to cope with his boss, the ruthless—and devastatingly attractive —Curt Dangerfield.

THE MAN ON HALF-MOON

BY

MARGARET WAY

MILLS & BOON LIMITED
17–19 FOLEY STREET
LONDON W1A 1DR

First published 1976
This edition 1977

© Margaret Way 1976

ISBN 0 263 72352 6

Made and printed in Great Britain by
Richard Clay (The Chaucer Press), Ltd., Bungay, Suffolk

CHAPTER ONE

THE banyan tree in the garden was colossal. A native of India, sacred to the Hindus, it filled Katharine with an increasing sense of unease. This was the 'singing' tree Darin had written her about. There couldn't be two of them. No native on the property would come near it, or camp anywhere beneath its jungle of prop roots that supported the great tree over a vast area. Forty feet up the main trunk were bark carvings—a man and a woman. The message was vivid and unmistakable. These were partners in a forbidden love pact. Both of them had died for it, victims of an ancient sorcery rite. No direct violence had been used on them. No marks had been found on the bodies. They had been struck down one week from the onset of their mysterious 'illness'. Image sorcery was the most powerful of all, and the tribes were notoriously magic-ridden.

It was Darin's belief that the guilty pair had probably starved themselves to death. Insatiably curious, very fit and adventurous, he had made the long climb, reporting that the drawings were still as clearly malignant as they had ever been. The whole business was long before his time in any case. Half-Moon was alive with legends and a fair sprinkling of horror stories, its history as colourful as it was fascinating. One of the biggest and earliest great Runs in the country, its name conjured up awe and respect from the most ardent city-dweller on the coastal fringe. Katharine, very new to it, felt overwhelmed.

Somewhere out there on that trackless wilderness, Darin was either dead or in terrible danger. The more she thought about it, the more sick and horrified she became, and the banyan tree was not helping any. Even in the crimson flush of sunset some subtle emanation of evil hovered over it. She shivered in the steamy heat, a powerful tenseness upon her. She was very pale and the soft grey of her eyes had darkened. I can't bear it, she thought. I can't bear it. Darin, my brother, and how little I know of him. She had never felt more terrifyingly alone in her life; the fragrance from the masses and masses of heliotrope bells on the vines of the veranda almost smothered her. She turned her head along the old squatter's chair and listened to the tumult of the birds, her silky blonde hair flowing palely over the dark green canvas. She was terribly, terribly tired, not even sure which world she was in. She could feel her body crying out for rest, but she couldn't relax. All her thoughts were given over to Darin and this flamboyantly beautiful wilderness, Half-Moon.

High over the lagoon, the birds were circling in their hundreds—white glittering corellas, black cockatoos with brilliant red tail feathers, the magpie geese, hawks and crows, the gorgeous enamelled

6

dress of the shrieking, excited parakeets, the paler, opal flash of the bigger parrots. Katharine had never seen so many birds nor witnessed such an incredibly beautiful sunset. It increased, if anything, her deep depression and sadness.

The sun threw a fiery red-gold light over everything: the fluttering wings, the great glassy sheet of water floating its waxen burden of lilies, the magnificent stands of paperbarks, the chalky white branches of the bush poplars, the casuarinas and the Zamia palms, the oddly angled pandanus and the dense grove of kapok trees. The bungalow was set in a thick grove of exotica. None of the flowers were familiar to her except the tall canna lilies, yellow and orange and speckled bronze. The tropics were ferociously beautiful, the steam and the heat and the impenetrable rain jungle that encroached on the station's borders. This was Arrow Head, the furthest outstation on the Run. Darin had been in charge of it for just six months.

Tears gathered in Katharine's eyes and she shifted her grip on the arm of the chair. Physical exhaustion was adding to her crushing weight of anxiety. This country was really rugged with its man-high grasses, its crocodiles and its snakes including the deadly taipan, but Darin was an experienced bushman. He had spent twelve of his twenty-seven years wandering the Outback. He had broken their widowed mother's heart when he had left home, straight out of school into a jackeroo's job on a Western station, completely alienating himself from their own way of life. Their mother had been shattered to lose the sight and support of her only son, her firstborn and her favourite. They had rarely seen Darin, but somehow or other he had kept up a spasmodic correspondence with his sister. Once after their mother died they had shared a vacation, but it was obvious that Darin's true love was the wild bush. Now it had claimed him. Hope was deserting her. It had been four days now.

Half-Moon was the headquarters and home station for a syndicate that owned properties from the Territory through to the Centre and out to the lush northern coastline of Queensland. The head of the syndicate was a man called Dangerfield. The name was well known in the pastoral world. The Dangerfields had been pioneers on the grand scale, and their holdings were extensive. At the time of his last letter, some two months before, Darin had been riding high in Dangerfield's favour. He had been appointed Manager of Arrow Head. The letter had been long and rambling, covering eight pages and full of strange hopes and plans. Katharine had been totally unprepared for news of her brother's disappearance. He had gone out unaccompanied on a shooting trip and never returned. What she did know was that Curt Dangerfield was a man terse to the point of cruelty—one telegram and one phone call had confirmed that. An arrogant, extremely high-handed man who expected to be obeyed, his whole attitude had been more of a vague censure than condolence. A search was being mounted. He,

Dangerfield, would keep her informed. Her presence on Half-Moon simply wasn't necessary. As Darin's sister, she had no real importance. Darin would be found—he hadn't said *dead or alive*, but that was what he implied. Was this the man Darin spoke of with such boundless admiration? It couldn't be. Katharine detested him already.

It was directly against his wishes to have come here at all, and it had proved both exhausting and expensive. More than two thousand miles and jolting, sickening, small trips to get to this isolated place. At least it had a landing strip neatly sliced out of the rich volcanic earth. Very likely a storm would break over her head, but Katharine didn't care. Darin was her brother. She had a right to be here no matter what Curt Dangerfield said. It would take courage to remain in this luxuriant, encroaching wilderness, but when she had slept she wouldn't feel so daunted. The deepening mystery of Darin. What had happened to him? He was well suited for this way of life, but it didn't take half an eye to see the dangers. A few months previously a stockman had been taken by a crocodile on an ill-advised swim in a lagoon. Others had become very ill after drinking 'sweet water' or attempting to live off 'bush tucker', the native roots and plants and wild fruit. The native stockmen and the myalls were friendly, the old days of nocturnal assaults were gone, but macabre things happened in isolated places. Men had been known to go mad with the heat and the loneliness, but Darin was young and

9

tough. He had much to live for, all sorts of plans. Some unguarded moment had laid him open for injury. He had left his horse, for the horse had returned to camp. Nothing worse could have happened to him than Katharine imagined.

She scarcely dared to sleep in case she had nightmares. A terrible anxiety was gnawing at her that wouldn't release its hold. The banyan tree, though the other trees rustled, was as still as death, and in the rapidly failing light it was easy to imagine it had some supernatural powers. Her delicate young face was sensitive and shadowed, fine-drawn by strain. No matter what Curt Dangerfield said, she would be here when they brought Darin in. It was her duty.

How their mother had loved him; though Darin always seemed so unaware of it. He had scarcely waited to be free of them and their lovely home, yet how far had she journeyed to bring him back again. The loving, tender streak was very apparent in Katharine, in her eyes and in her mouth and the sweet, soft, cadence of her voice. In her short life only Curt Dangerfield had so painfully elicited her hostility. She recognised him for what he was—the most ruthless man she had ever had contact with. Darin's confidences had been all wrong.

The brief purple twilight had fallen. In a short time it would be night and she would be alone in this primitive Eden except for a very gentle and elderly aboriginal stockman and his two boys. She could still see their glossy brown faces framed in horrified surprise from the moment she had arrived. She had literally dropped from the skies, shocking them into a state of upheaval—a white woman, young, and as fair as a lotus lily. It made no difference that she was Darin's sister; it wasn't fitting or suitable that she should be here. By now the enterprising old gentleman had probably radioed Half-Moon with his most unwelcome piece of news. Dangerfield would be furious. His voice alone was sufficient indication that he had never been crossed in his life, for all its hard charm.

Inside, the small bungalow was surprisingly comfortable; living and dining as a single unit with inbuilt seating, swing doors through to a tiny kitchen, the shower room beyond, and a small bedroom that nevertheless was good enough for a motel. Even striped cotton curtains were massed at the windows for sun control. Someone had taken the trouble to make this place hospitable. Lights blossomed at the flick of a switch from their own generator and Katharine's eyes scanned again the long rows of books, literary and sheer escapism. Darin had grown up in a beautiful, traditional old home, but he obviously found this place more inspiring. He had never been much of a one for books, but the nights would be long.

Darin was an adventurer by nature. He had needed no help in deciding his life. Ever since he had been a small boy the vast Outback had been there calling him; its dangers and discomforts, its vast distances, the heart-shaking loneliness. This was the Big Sky Country for Darin, impregnated with magic. The woman influence in his life had been banished early. Or had it? For somewhere behind Darin's last rambling letter, Katharine sensed the existence of a special woman. Darin had referred to no one, yet the whole tone of the letter was inflamed, swept by some passion. It now seemed vital to find out if Darin had indeed become involved with someone. In an isolated place like this, it wouldn't be difficult to find out.

Katharine walked about the bungalow a little aimlessly, toying with this latest theory. Darin was very good-looking, like a sleek, tawny cat—her own colouring deepened many, many times. Aggressively masculine, he was conversely very attractive to women. The fact that he wanted no woman striding at his side meant nothing. A woman with a purpose could accomplish anything. The flesh could be moved by a sudden storm even if the brain couldn't. Darin had a fiery temperament, but his way wasn't marriage. Yet despite this, Katharine found herself convinced Darin had succumbed to some temptation called woman. The woman's name she would find out, though she had nothing to go on as yet, but her own intuition.

Lost in her thoughts, she was nearly frightened out of her skin by the sudden appearance of a man in the open doorway.

'Nervous, miss?' The man stepped in and the light fell over his face. He was brawny and bearded with an obstinate, rather dangerous look.

'You startled me!' Slowly her heart began to beat more regularly.

The man grinned and swept off his wide-brimmed hat. 'Dusty, miss. Dusty Fisher.'

'You weren't here when I arrived,' she said faintly.

'Just got back!' He smiled and gave her a bold up-and-down look with his prominent, pale blue eyes.

She realised immediately he was no person she could stand about talking to. 'I'm Katharine Sutton,' she supplied as though it was armour, looking over his broad shoulders for some non-existent aid.

'Yes, I know.' Momentarily his eyes narrowed. 'Sorry about old Darin. Not like him to lose himself. Reckon he knows this place as much as anyone outside the Boss.'

'I'm very worried about him!' Katharine said bluntly. They both knew secretly that he repelled her, but it was adding to Dusty's odd excitement.

'I believe you.' His eyes were all over her, her skin and her long blonde hair, her slender form, reflecting his peculiar admiration.

'It was kind of you to come up and speak to me, Mr Fisher,' she said repressively.

'Want me to fix you somethin' to eat?'

'No, thank you!' She nearly sprang to the door, scarcely able to contemplate such lunacy. 'I'll find something for myself. I'm very tired.'

He shrugged his muscular shoulders, the concen-

13

tration in his pale eyes absolute. 'I want you to know I'll be all the help I can.'

The isolation of the place was enormous and inescapable. 'Thank you.' Her tone was as cool and dismissive as she judged it wise to be.

Dusty, however, was in a very sociable mood, his blue eyes glowing. 'I'll say this for you Suttons—you're lookers! Darin never told me he had a little beauty for a sister.'

'Did he mention me at all?' she asked dryly.

'Can't say he did!' Dusty smiled half chidingly. 'Mentioned his mum once or twice. Always on to him to make somethin' of himself. University graduate and all that!'

'I have an arts degree,' she said calmly. 'It didn't hurt me.'

'A girl like you has got enough!' He was almost leering at her, making no attempt to move off.

A situation was arising that she dreaded and it was rapidly worsening. His square, strong hand suddenly shot out and patted her shoulder, lingering along her upper arm. Anger and a flash of panic almost held Katharine paralysed, but she couldn't afford to lose her control and incite him further. Her crystal-grey eyes looked back at him steadily. 'Take your hand off my arm. Would you mind leaving?'

'Would I mind leaving?' He mimicked her polished accent, but there was nothing vaguely funny about him. He looked stupid and empty of scruple. 'Here I was thinkin' you might like company.' His raw-boned hand tangled in her hair. 'Soft like silk,' he said thickly. 'I was forgettin'!'

Katharine jerked her head away painfully. 'The only company I want, Mr Fisher,' she said icily, 'is my brother's.'

'Oh, sure!' His eyes lingered on her mouth oppressively. 'I haven't seen a girl like you in years. You're my idea of an angel!'

'Then I'd hate to spoil it. If you don't go away I'll call for the others. They're not too far away.'

She could see he was getting angry; his wide mouth curled. 'What's your idea comin' up here anyway?' he demanded.

'I should think that was obvious. To find my brother!'

'*You* find him? Hell!' His contempt was complete. 'You couldn't ~~get~~ past the front gate. You wouldn't survive for a minute. You need someone with experience. I've had years in the bush. You ought to be nice to me.'

'Why, particularly?' she asked, contemptuous herself.

'Because I fancy you,' he said tonelessly. 'I hold the view your brother's dead.'

Her skin whitened to transparency. 'And what about Mr Dangerfield?'

'Dangerfield's a very important man.'

'I won't argue with that.'

'He doesn't ruddy well know you're here!' He almost spat at her, full of an ugly mixture of malice and desire.

'What makes you think *that*?' Ironically she was now clinging to Dangerfield as her protector. This repulsive brute wasn't so devoid of intelligence that he couldn't sober abruptly at a name.

'I can take a good guess,' he said grimly. 'You wouldn't *be* here, little lady. Mr Dangerfield's got very definite ideas. He's a person of character, a fine gentleman. He wouldn't want no woman out here, not alone. Never! Not a girl with shining eyes and long blonde hair. You travel with me, little girl, and you'll be well looked after. We may even find your brother. I got a few clues!'

The ugly recklessness was upon him again that almost but not quite silenced her.

'Mr Dangerfield will be here in the morning.'

He shot her a searing look. 'You're makin' that up.'

'She isn't!'

A voice behind them brought Dusty back to the present.

'No business here, Dusty!' the old aboriginal stockman said, his voice soft and smooth, his dark face impassive. 'As Missy said, the Boss'll be here in the mornin'. Meantimes, *I'm* in charge!'

Dusty swore violently, deeply chagrined. 'That'll be the day, ya black devil.'

'A black man is as good as a white man with the Boss. Want to check on it, Dusty? The Boss is in a nice mood.'

'No, thanks.' Even Dusty was struck with that one. 'What else are his orders?'

16

'See Missy is safe and comfortable.'

'I suppose he's angry,' Katharine demanded, looking exhausted enough to drop.

'Well ...' The old stockman made a funny little gesture that conveyed a blistering wrath. 'He was tipped off in any case. Ain't no one out here would withhold information. When I got through meself he already had the message. Can't land here at night, otherwise he would. Shouldn'a come here, missy.'

'I want to know what's happened to my brother,' Katharine said doggedly, knowing full well how rash she had been.

'The Boss'll handle all that,' old Barney offered gravely.

'He may be your boss, but lord knows he's not mine!' Katharine responded, almost swaying on her feet.

'You haven't met him,' Dusty shot in maliciously. 'Make a damn nuisance of yourself and you'll find yourself back in the city. It's a habit of Dangerfield's, callin' the play!'

Katharine shook her blonde head and turned away. Two thousand miles distant she had thought she knew best, but this pagan place was too much. Barney came up to her, true kindness in his liquid black eyes.

'You're tuckered out, missy. Have no fears about anythin'. The Boss trust me. *You* trust me.'

'I do, thank you, Barney.' She turned to smile at him and Dusty drew in his breath.

'Let's shove off together.'

'That's a good idea, Dusty,' the old aboriginal said amiably. 'I'll be posted right outside your door, missy, for all of the night. Sleep easy.'

'Aren't you bein' a bit damn silly?' Dusty demanded belligerently.

'Jes' followin' orders!'

Despite Barney's armed presence outside her door and the Boss's O.K. to 'shoot that fool Fisher, if you have to!' Katharine slept badly, the long hours of consciousness, of heat and mosquitoes, punctuated by nightmares. The first rays of dawn light brought in the worst one. She was lost in an unfamiliar world, held captive in the jungle mesh of the great banyan. Birds were screeching in the breathless air; strange birds with brilliant plumage and striking beaks, their scarlet crowns ruffled like headdresses, their glittering eyes like bright yellow glass buttons. These were the birds of the tropical rain forest and their home was the banyan tree. The largest of them, a great rainbow-coloured parrot, dived for her, its beak full of figs. She threw herself back against a prop root and covered her eyes. She knew it was a dream, but she couldn't fight out of it. She couldn't even scream, drugged with this dream terror that refused to let go.

From somewhere a voice reached her, calling her name. It was dark-timbred, distinctive, calling from close range. Katharine braced herself, her agitation extreme. It *had* to be Darin, like her, a captive of the great banyan tree. She choked on his name, imploring him. It wasn't air she was breathing, but a thick blanketing fog. 'Darin!' she screamed.

Hands gripped her, cased in iron, and finally she was coming out of it. This wasn't Darin; this was the enemy. She brought up her own hands, the nails curling protectively like talons. She could feel her body wrenched, the sharp stab of pain that ran down her neck. She felt dizzy, her heart beating rapidly. The voice was persistent, the lean fingers cool and strong. 'Oh, Darin ...' she said his name again, knowing he had truly slipped away from her. The hands that were holding her hurt.

'Snap out of it!' the voice said, simply trying to get through to her.

She shook back her long hair and opened her eyes. It was a curious sensation, knowing what he looked like.

'Where is he?' she said painfully. 'Where's Darin?'

'Good God!' He stood up beside her, looking down at her as if she were an oddity—a tall, very commanding-looking man. His crisply curling helmet of hair was almost ebony, his skin like dark copper, and the eyes that were looking at her so intently were as chilly and impenetrable as steel, only they were green. His chin was cleft and his shapely mouth was hard and firm. He had no sense of humour.

She gave a soft, rather strangled little laugh, the

dawn wind through the open doorway fanning her hot cheeks. She had put him through a bad time. There was nothing worse than a hysterical woman. She didn't blame him for looking green daggers. 'I'm sorry,' she said. 'You didn't give me a chance to come out of it myself.'

'What was I supposed to do?' he asked abruptly. 'Stand by while you thrashed about like a terror-stricken child? What on God's earth persuaded you to ignore sound advice? I thought I made it abundantly clear to you that this was no place for a woman. And you're not even that. How old *are* you?'

'Twenty-two.' There was a darkening area on the fine skin of her wrists and she rubbed them gingerly. The imprint of his thumb was quite clear.

'Incredible!' he said as though she was utterly feckless, and not to be held responsible for her actions. He moved away from her, his back to her, framed in the doorway. Even his back looked ruthless, Katharine thought. He wore slacks and a khaki bush shirt and somehow made such an outfit look perfect. She had slept on the living room sofa in her cream and black printed T-shirt and her cream slacks, and both of them were crushed. She lifted herself up on to one elbow and ran her fingers through her long blonde hair. He didn't seem in the least disposed to say any more, just stared out over the awakening lagoon, a frown on his dark, handsome face. They were mutually antagonistic—just another queer trick of Fate.

'Surely you understand that I want to find Darin?

You haven't answered my question.'

'There's no answer as yet!' he said coolly, turning to glance at her face.

'From a man like you I can't accept that.'

He rounded on her instantly, his metallic green gaze resting on her with such a degree of intensity that she lowered her head. He shook her—his whole style, his looks and his manner. She would have a hard time achieving just such a crisp tone again. 'This place,' she offered almost apologetically, 'that tree out there, the banyan, it makes me nervous.'

Obviously he didn't share her misgivings, for one black eyebrow lifted. 'This is the most beautiful place in the world, Miss Sutton,' he said calmly as though her whole pattern of behaviour was totally irrational, 'and it's mine!'

'Some day someone might take it off you!' she found herself saying.

'*No.*'

'No, perhaps not!' she repeated after him with something like melancholy. 'Yet it's a secret place— eerie, the birds and the blossoming. A flowering, ruined world.'

'You've too much imagination!' He sounded very emphatic. 'And you're not yet in charge of your own emotions.'

'Some day soon, I might be!' she said, her hair falling in a shining, protective stream around her small, finely modelled head. 'Where could Darin have gone?'

'He *said* on a shooting trip.'

Some note in his dark, sombre voice made her tremble. 'You don't believe that?'

'Let's say my doubts are increasing.'

He was so tall she had to tilt her head to look up to him, yet she felt for the moment incapable of getting to her feet. 'Perhaps you'll tell me what you do think?'

'Maybe after breakfast.'

'Why, there's very little here,' she said vaguely.

'Not here,' he said, and his smile didn't reach his eyes. 'Half-Moon.'

'I don't know that I'm coming.'

'Don't be absurd. You're coming all right, though you'll never admit you were wrong to come here in the first place.'

'It would have been impossible for me to remain behind. Darin is my brother. I wish I didn't have to keep reminding you of the fact.'

'You'll only suffer,' he said in an attacking kind of voice, flickering flames in his very green eyes.

'My dream, my nightmare has upset me. I don't care what you say, this place has a strange desolation upon it.'

'You sound such a child!' He glanced down rather harshly at her, irritated more than anything by her curious impression of fragility, the white skin, the faint blue veins showing at her temples, the long, palely glittering hair, the clear pure grey of her thickly lashed eyes. It could be so easily done to pack her up and send her home again, yet the lost look in her beautiful silvery eyes altered his intention. Life hadn't been easy for her, would never be easy for her, with that sensitive, softly sensuous mouth, and for her to have encountered that savage, Fisher! Appalling the situations women got themselves in to, and this one was just a child sent to plague him.

'Are you capable of getting up off that sofa?' he asked her. 'I have to get back again. I've a million things to attend to that your sudden arrival messed up.'

A curious expression rippled across her face, a mixture of pain and a strange antagonism. 'Maybe it's *you* who's messed things up, Mr Dangerfield. You're Darin's employer, yet he's still missing. This is a big country, but people don't just disappear!' In a sharp turn she came to her feet, her hair swinging like silver-gilt.

'Perhaps Darin's got plans of his own,' he pointed out in a controlled yet recognizably cold voice.

'Then tell me?' she pleaded. 'I wish you wouldn't talk like this.'

'Are you ready to come back with me?' was all he said.

'I haven't the energy to resist.'

'Nor anything else. At the moment you're properly mixed up.'

Something in his expression, the green eyes as they rested upon her, made her heart constrict. 'Have you a heart, Mr Dangerfield?'

'No, I haven't!'

'I believe you.' She gave a little, shaky laugh.

23

'Then you're learning.'

'How typical, and I don't mean it as a compliment. There could be no *Mrs* Dangerfield.'

'I could easily arrange it.'

'One could only feel sorry,' she managed, not caring.

'What's on your mind, Miss Sutton?' he asked her, and the harshness of his tone shocked her.

'I'm not doing the right thing.'

'*Now* you're discovering!' he said without hesitation. 'Look, I'm quite sure,' he said more kindly, 'there's nothing sinister in Darin's disappearance. It's my own theory he's simply gone off. He wasn't managing at all well lately.'

'But that's impossible!'

'*Is* it?'

There was immense authority about him that made Katharine feel helpless, so that almost for a moment she half believed in his theory herself. His eyes, in sharp contrast to the dark tan of his face, were fixed on her searchingly.

'When did you last hear from him?'

'I told you when you first rang me,' she said desperately. 'Two months ago.'

'Exactly about the time when things started to go wrong.'

'I don't believe you. I can't!'

He turned his back on her as if to escape her. 'Make us a cup of coffee. We'll eat later.'

Gentle as Katharine's nature was, he awoke something wild in her. 'Tell me *now*!' She caught at his

24

arm, this splendid example of an autocrat, this man with his wealth and his background, his unassailable aura. He wasn't her kind of person and it was a mistake to touch him. She felt him stiffen, the brilliant green gaze first on her hand, then her face. If she had been given to prodigious imaginings she would have said some torrent of feeling, quite alien, flared between them, and foolishly she felt frightened.

'I'm sorry,' she said, and her hand fell away from him.

She was completely unaware, even indifferent to her own beauty, he could see that; strands of her gleaming, loose hanging hair trailed over his sleeve like soft silk. She did not know herself and she certainly did not know her brother. The look in her pure grey eyes gave him an unfamiliar stab of compunction so that he smiled at her. It didn't last long, but as a smile it was memorable. 'Please, *Katharine*, may I? Don't go on thinking I'm ruthlessly suppressing information. I'm doing everything I can to locate Darin's exact whereabouts. He's an exceptional and experienced bushman. I can't accept that he's lost, and we've combed a vast area. I'll never let go until I do find him. In the meantime, since you've involved yourself in the immediate situation, you'll come back to Half-Moon with me. In a way you've provoked your own crisis coming up here.'

'It was essential,' she said in a soft, dedicated voice.

His brief laugh underlined his powerful disbelief. 'Have it your own way, for the moment. Are you going to make the coffee, or am I?'

'I can see it will make it a lot easier if I do what I'm told.'

'Be sure of it. It will save time.'

It was no use pretending she could ever like him, and the sudden sparkle in her grey eyes told him. 'I'll do it,' she said, walking away from him, her pale hair keeping her face hidden. She had stranded herself in this beautiful violent place. The marks of Curt Dangerfield's hands on her arms were already turning to bruises. She walked into the tiny kitchen and began to make the coffee. Only one thing stopped her from crying. He had said that he wouldn't rest until he had found Darin and she believed that he would keep his promise. He was that kind of man. In coming to Half-Moon at all she had placed herself directly into his hands.

'Give me five minutes,' he called briefly. 'I'm gong to speak to the men.'

Katharine welcomed his sudden departure and didn't even answer. The water would take a little time to boil and she wanted to freshen herself up. Inexplicably the bedroom mirror told her that instead of looking tired and tense, her skin had colour in it and her eyes were as clear as crystal. Her long disarranged hair glinted in the light. She leaned over quickly and combed it. There was not a thing she could do about her clothes. She would have to start out on her journey just the way she was.

By the time Curt Dangerfield returned she had

the coffee ready for him, moving very delicately and precisely in the confined area so as to avoid touching him. The merest contact with this man had the power to shake her. He lifted the cup and drank it very hot, no milk. He was his own man and there was a decided air of strain between them. She watched him finish his drink, the shapely mouth, the square, cleft chin. He looked up quickly and pinned her gaze. He was a man of influence and he was used to manipulating people.

'You don't like me, Katharine, do you?' His voice had a biting edge to it.

'We're not the same kind of people.'

'Now where in the world did you learn that?'

'You're a very disturbing man,' she put forward discreetly.

'Go ahead. Anything else?'

'At the moment it's more than my life's worth.'

'You mean you *need* me.'

'It's vitally important to me that you find Darin.'

'*Darin*,' he said harshly in a curious reaction. 'Drink up that coffee and stop dithering.'

'I'm too tense,' she said flatly.

'You don't look it. You look incredibly soft and sheltered, just a beautiful little girl in a sad dream. The crying fits haven't shadowed your eyes, even so you don't seem to be able to stop your hand shaking.'

'Does anyone dare disagree with you?' she asked bitterly.

'Don't look so upset about it. You employ some pretty neat little tactics yourself.'

'Family loyalty, commitment, is very important.'

'You have your life. Darin has his.'

'Darin is *lost*!' Katharine had the weird notion she was talking to herself. 'Don't you see that?'

His green eyes were narrowed, just staring at her. 'I'm checking on it, Katharine, but the thought's not keeping me awake.'

She flung up her hand in a tragic little gesture and he caught it, bearing it down again, holding it firmly against the cool, dark wood of the table. 'I said I'll help you and I will. Darin just didn't measure up. In the last few months he was no good at all.'

'I just can't accept that. You're not talking about Darin at all.'

'How well did you know him?' he asked her, and his voice chilled her. Oddly it was a very attractive voice with a dangerous ability to awake all kinds of sensations. 'I've had a fair enough picture from Darin. From all accounts he never saw eye to eye with your mother. Neither did he appear to worry unduly about his sister.'

'That's none of your business!'

'It is. You've made it my business. Maybe Darin will leave a few of his tracks uncovered. Relax, Katharine, relax.' His voice was edgy but not unkind. 'How long have you been on your own?'

'Since my mother died. Afterwards Darin and I shared a holiday. That was four years ago.'

28

'I don't understand you,' he mused. 'In many ways Darin gave you and your mother a rough deal. Explain to me why you love him?'

'I just do. He's all I've got.'

'Not *you*. You're a special kind of girl. You could have any man you want!'

'I don't want any man at all. I just want to find my brother, to know he's safe. He wrote to me, full of plans, engrossed in them. Nothing adds up!'

'Cry and I'll start off without you.'

Her eyes flashed, shimmering with life, a young girl's face, but with delicate strength and courage. 'I'd make out.'

He only smiled, many unspoken things between them. 'A wonderful piece of bravado! Growing up is painful, Katharine. Perhaps you've been sheltered too long. Come now, collect your things, it's time we left. We'll have a rain-storm before the day's over. The monsoon isn't far off.'

Under the banyan tree, she almost took fright again, breathless with a burden of presentiments she could not understand. The dawn that had been so still and colourless suddenly erupted into life. The heavy weight of branches exploded with birds, not singing birds, but shrieking, squabbling, a mad crescendo of sound, colouring the curve of the sun with their brilliant scarlet and cobalt, bright yellow and green. A giant fig fell from the tree and stabbed into her hair, and she recoiled against Curt Dangerfield's arm, her cheek touching his sleeve.

'Oh!' Her long-drawn shuddering sigh betrayed

her agitation. *He* belonged in this place as the great banyan belonged to the tropics, but she felt a welling disorientation. The rising sun spread a golden glow over her white skin, gold washed her grey eyes, but there was a soft desolation in their clear depths.

His hand came down on her shoulder, his voice as crisp and bracing as though directed towards an over-imaginative child. 'Stop that! The tree's a freak, I'll grant you, but don't go crediting it with a presence!'

'It appals me,' she said truthfully. 'It's no ordinary tree, I'm sure. There's something brooding about it, unapproachable.'

He made a small jeering sound, intensely male, very hard and alert, as he propelled her out of the deep well of gloom into full sunlight. 'What do you do in the city, Katharine? What sort of job?'

'I'm a teacher,' she said simply.

'Good grief.'

'I graduated with a first class diploma.'

'You don't look very scholarly to me. Nor wise!'

'I happen to be good at my job, Mr Dangerfield,' she said quietly. 'My girls like me.'

'God knows I think I like you myself!'

'Then you may have noticed I'm not able to respond.'

'How fascinating! Let's try to keep it that way, shall we?'

There was a cool sensuality to his face she had never noticed before. It bewildered her, making her feel shatteringly aware of him. 'I suppose that was very rude of me?'

'To be fair, yes, Katharine. You seem such a good little girl, too. However, we've both given one another fair warning. Interesting, isn't it?'

'I don't usually come right out and say what I think,' she said slowly, talking as much to herself as to him. This was true and she had no desire to be unpleasant. It was so ill-bred. 'I'm in a strange mood, I think!'

'Precisely.'

'Nothing is as it should be!' Her voice was vaguely tormented, and unexpectedly his hand came under her chin tipping her face to him.

'Why didn't you leave it to the professionals, like I told you?'

'You'll never understand,' she said, trying to turn her face away.

Apparently this angered him. 'Don't you think I know how you feel?' he asked harshly.

'No.' She shook her blonde head. 'I don't think you've ever truly cared for anyone in your life.'

'You seem to have learned that in a very short time.'

'Is it true?' she demanded of him, her grey eyes enormous in her delicate face.

'Let it lie, Katharine!' he said tautly. 'All you *do* have to know is, I promised I'd help you and I will.'

'You've *got* to!'

'Then try to be a bit cleverer. Your dislike of me appears to have leaked out.'

'I'm sorry I said it!' she apologised.

'You can't have it both ways.'

Swamped by his aura, she broke away from him, moving swiftly through the front gate like a swaying flower on a long stalk. 'I write children's books too,' she tossed over her shoulder in an effort to lessen the tension.

'Get paid for it?' He caught up with her easily, a faint smile softening his mouth.

'No.' She smiled herself. 'Not much anyway, but it's early days.'

'Being up here might help a great deal,' he rejoined suavely. 'Your horizons need broadening. You're far too inhibited.'

'Perhaps I am—by your standards.' She threw up her slender arms in a curiously embracing, tender gesture. 'It's all so heady, unfamiliar. The sights and sounds, the musky scent of the trees and the flowers —primitive really. The environment must affect one. Even the air is different. It shimmers, it's colour-stained. The birds are fantastic, every tree splashed with their plumage, and finally the feeling that the rains are coming.'

'So they are. We're on the verge of the Wet. The heat can get pretty intense, suffocating really. Being cool-skinned, you'll emerge like a lily.'

His sidelong glance, greenly sardonic, still affected her strangely. He was at one with the lushness and brilliance, the danger in the blossoming wildernes. She was the outsider. And Darin. The very thought of his name stirred the joy and pain of

32

nostalgia. Hers had been a lonely childhood. She had only Darin and he had left her scarcely before he had grown to be a man, but she remembered what fun he had been, his careless affection, the way he had occasionally sheltered her from their mother's shifting moods. She had been grateful for Darin, but her image of him, invariably, was not the true image of the man. The circumstances of her childhood, her lonely adolescence, had coloured her vision. Adventurous, carefree, tawny to her silvery fairness, Darin was her own private possession. Where her mother had grown bitter, Katharine's love for her absentee brother had never diminished.

She turned to look at Curt Dangerfield, a virtual stranger, but taking a hard, proprietorial line in her life. His profile had the remote beauty of sculpture, but when he turned his dark head his eyes were brilliantly alive. She had no time to think of anything but what was directly on her mind.

'I'm almost afraid to ask you,' she said, 'but did you *like* Darin?'

'He had a position of trust in my employ.'

'That's not what I asked.'

'Let us say, Katharine, I liked Darin well enough —at the beginning. Does that answer your question?'

'Rather cruelly, I'm afraid. But then I knew that about you. From the beginning.'

'In a fraction of the usual time,' he conceded. 'Yet I seem to have taken pity on you.'

'But I don't need it or want it, Mr Dangerfield!'

She had never spoken to anyone like this before, such a mixture of heat and defiance and a terrible, prickling awareness.

'Don't evade the truth!' he said curtly. 'Face it. You're young and defenceless. God, you should see yourself asleep! Someone has to shield you. You're out of your depth here.'

'Yes,' she said as the thought swept her. 'Sometimes a man's strength is everything. All I can do is grow another skin.'

'You can't beat satin,' he said, and his eyes touched every bit of her skin.

The flicker in his green eyes disturbed her profoundly. 'If anything the birds are arguing more fiercely,' she said, swiftly refocusing her gaze. 'Not a one of them in harmony.'

'Are any of us?'

'I've led a very peaceful life up to date.'

'I've a feeling, Katharine, that all that will be changing.'

She shivered a little, evading his searching eyes. He was clever and ruthless and he could lay claim to striking good looks. She felt like a child, weaponless, incapable of a mature judgment. What would be the result of her time on Half-Moon? The green wilderness and the rain-forest extended as far as she could see. Only Dangerfield stood between her and it. Last night she had passed in an atmosphere of menace, for all old Barney's presence outside her door. She had placed herself at incredible risk, damning herself in Dangerfield's eyes as both stupid and hysterical. Now that she was here, it seemed to her almost a fantastic venture. This wasn't her background, the meticulous and orderly, the cool elegance and comfort of her own small apartment, the graceful, mellow surroundings of the excellent girls' school she had attended for many long years herself. This was the wild bush, a primitive enchantment.

In the bright sunlight her hair turned to ash-gold. Dangerfield's eyes flickered over her, brilliant, inscrutable. 'If you want to, Katharine, you can hold my hand.'

'Do I look that lost?' she asked.

'Yes.'

'This is an irresistible atmosphere. I, too, may disappear.'

He loomed very tall beside her, his handsome face severe. 'How do you imagine that could happen when I'll be right here beside you?'

'To be honest, I don't know why you're allowing me to stay at all.'

'It certainly wasn't my intention before I arrived.'

They were staring at each other—he, very hard and sure of himself, she, a flush over her cheekbones and her grey eyes troubled.

'So you feel sorry for me?' she demanded.

'Any objection?'

'It's not kindness, I'm sure.'

'Self-interest, Katherine. Your remarkable woman's mind has already told you that.'

'I won't be upsetting your household in any way?

I know nothing of you except the little Darin wrote me. Ironically he thought a great deal of you—almost a hero figure.'

'Instead of a megalomaniac?'

'I never implied that!' she said, quite shocked.

'Oh, come on,' he said, all of a sudden vastly irritated. 'You're nearly shaking with fright!'

'It isn't that. You're alien to me, Mr Dangerfield. So is this place.'

'Strangely, young Katharine, you quite dazzle me.' He spoke crisply, looking at her with apparent dislike. Then he turned and stalked away from her to the waiting Cessna, very tall and lithe, covering the distance in complete silence, with Katharine hurrying, hot and uncomfortable, trying to keep up with him. Nearing the light aircraft, he hesitated, but only for a moment.

Probably thinking of taking off without me, Katharine wondered. She would have to guard her tongue. In Curt Dangerfield's presence it had become uncommonly ready.

'Don't get carried away,' he said as she came up to him, breathing rather quickly. 'I won't go without you.'

'It had crossed my mind.'

'Mine as well. One can only guess what might happen to you.'

She shuddered, thinking of Fisher.

'Little fool!' he said, reading her thoughts accurately. 'Don't you see how things can be for a woman?'

'How they've always been.'

'Sometimes a woman is more precious than gold.'

'Not to you.'

'I keep my fancies hidden.' He gave her a mocking, brilliant grin, his teeth very white and even.

'Has not a one influenced you?' she asked curiously.

'My grandmother.'

'Surely another?'

'I wouldn't like all my past affairs to gang up on me. But no, young Katharine, not really.'

An unfamiliar excitement seemed to pour into the air. Katharine felt it acutely. She made for the Cessna, the nape of her neck shivering. Vaguely it came to her that Curt Dangerfield could play on a woman like a violin. His was a masterly hand, but she wanted no part of him other than to find Darin. His hands at her waist set her nerves at a clamour. Nothing he did was expected. He half lifted her, half pushed her into the aircraft. An impossible man. A dragon, his warm breath on her cheek.

'There, you can quiver beside me. Strap yourself in.'

Full of incomprehensible yearnings, she did what she was told. A thousand years from now she would still try to escape this man.

She looked at him uncertainly, but he was now ignoring her, his dark golden profile empty of awareness. Women created only a very small stir in his life. Fleetingly but not seriously she almost wished it might have been different. But common sense, of which she had plenty, asserted itself. Curt Dangerfield carried with him an aura of dynamism, and in its wake would come pain. Once again she remembered she was out of her depth, warning bells in her head gently tolling. The sun bounced savagely off the wing and momentarily she shut her eyes.

The aircraft burst into life and moved slowly forward. Barney and the two young aboriginal stockmen suddenly appeared and Dangerfield slid back the window and waved to them; fresh air rushed into the overheated cabin. Katharine in turn smiled and waved while the man beside her completed his last-minute checks, then opened the throttle wide. The light aircraft responded and Katharine could feel herself bracing as it went forward, faster and faster, until finally it lifted sweetly and neatly, soaring into the imperious, sun-drenched air. Blue sky was above and beneath them, the noise of the engine died back to a drone.

'No, don't unstrap yourself. Just a safety precaution.'

'That was effortless!' she murmured with evident relief.

'I hope so. I've had my licence a long time.'

'And I think you love it. Am I right?'

'Look around us. Sky. Sky. Sky. Of course I love it!'

Far beneath them was the luxuriant jungle, a river cutting a silver slice through it. Dangerfield was holding the aircraft beautifully steady. Others before them had plummeted into the rain-forest, but Katharine felt no shade of fear. She had, she realised, complete confidence in him.

He touched her arm and pointed out a tumbling waterfall, a purple-slashed ravine like an ancient temple. Seen from the sky the whole landscape was incredibly awesome yet startlingly beautiful as well. Moon-shaped lakes and lagoons glittered, then in the distance a great clearing, moving heads of stock. They flew over the rich river flats and she looked down at them, her breath quickening.

'It must be an odd feeling to own immense tracts of land?'

'Somehow I don't think of that part of it at all,' he said. 'My family, our shareholders, work as a team.'

'You're the boss.'

'There has to be one, Katharine.'

'Yes, of course. A boss is essential.'

'Don't go thinking it's all glamour. It's a hard life in many ways.'

'With plenty of rewards. However did you cut your way through this wild, tropical bushland?'

'You can read about it if you like. There are plenty of Dangerfield graves about.'

'Then you're rightly called pioneers.'

'It's our life.'

'Maybe it's proved calamitous for Darin,' she suggested.

'This is the first incidence of a man disappearing that I've struck. We've had accidents, fatalities, shootings, stampedes, grudges that won't be settled, but we've never had anything that could be called a mystery. Perhaps Darin is trying to draw attention to himself?'

'Why ever would he want to do that?' she asked.

'Unlike you with your fastidious little air of reserve, Darin has rather a flamboyant personality.'

'Nothing in this wide world would make me believe he's doing this on purpose.'

His voice was hard to the point of curtness. 'Perhaps you don't know him as well as you should?'

'You have no regard for my feelings, have you?'

'You can stand a few home truths, surely? Except for a slight family resemblance, it's imposible to link you with Darin at all. Darin is quite capable of looking after himself with a shrewd eye to the main chance, but you—! Why, you're such a babe you throw me off balance.'

'How wonderful! I imagine very few people have done that!'

'No one up here is fresh out of the nursery.'

His mockery hit her like a dart. She turned her face away, pale hair falling like a curtain. 'I acted for the best possible reasons. Please don't look about for another motive.'

'My dear child, would I do that? You're purity itself!'

And you're the most hateful, unsettling man I've ever met. She would have been shocked to know that he read her thoughts in her small, whitening knuckles.

He gave her a brief, acknowledging burst of

laughter and judged it a good idea to change the subject. 'That vivid green patch down there,' he said very casually, 'is true, optimum rain-forest, luxuriant, diverse and supporting a complex plant and animal community. Not all our rain-forests are the same. There are upland, lowland monsoon forests, but they're all north of the tropic of Capricorn. Rain-forests only occur in equatorial regions, Central and South America, the Amazon basin, the Congo basin, and the Indo-Malaysian regions, to which our own rain-forests and the rain-forests of New Guinea are most closely related. The great open stretches, more golden than green, are the woodlands. They separate the forests much as the sea separates islands. All the brilliantly coloured patches, the pink and white, the orange and scarlet, are the flowering trees.'

'I'm fortunate to see it this way,' she said evenly.

'Yes, you are. Most people only see the rain-forest floor. You'll notice that the canopy is slightly uneven. That was cyclone Tracy, the same one that devastated Darwin. Torrential rains and maximum force winds weaken the root system and bring down the giants. The babies of the forest are at least a hundred feet tall.'

'It looks a fascinating place even from this distance.'

'On the ground it can be overwhelming,' he told her, 'The rain-forest has an atmosphere all its own. Man is the invader. The forest floor is warm and humid, a green gloom, and the growth is prolific.

41

The giant trees are covered with other plants, the mosses and ferns and the orchids, great cascading sprays of them. Everything is on the grand scale, the world's tallest palms and tree ferns, the sheer drops of the waterfalls. Even when a storm is lashing the tops of the trees the rain only trickles to the ground. The most brilliant sunshine cannot pierce the canopy. In some places it's so dark only specially adapted plants grow there. Everything reaches for the light, the trees and the climbers, the strangler vines, gigantic ropes of them seemingly hanging from nowhere, real Tarzan stuff and very characteristic of rainforests. The staghorns and the elkhorns are magnificent. They attach themselves to just about every tree bark. Then there are the unique cauliflories, flowering rain-forest trees, only the flowers, in great bunches, stud the trunks. They start off a few inches from the ground and star the bark up to a good fifty feet or more. Most spectacular.'

'And the orchids?'

'Well, the orchids, Katharine,' he said, his eyes touching her, 'are extremely beautiful and some of them vaguely sinister. The fact they are protected doesn't stop visitors in our National Parks stripping the trees to a height of forty feet. They can't seem to keep their hands off them. Selling the orchids and ferns from the rain-forest is a pretty lucrative business.'

'I've heard the same about the birds.'

'Smuggling is illegal,' he said grimly, 'but it still goes on. The coastline is extremely difficult to patrol and a lot leave the country by way of Cape York. Smugglers will try anything. Plenty of air travellers have been caught stowing drugged birds away in suitcases and box cameras and even in the lining of their clothes. Customs picked up a woman the other day when a brilliantly coloured feather suddenly shot out the neck of her jacket. The beautiful little finches aren't safe, neither are the butterflies. There are more up here in the rain-forest than the rest of Australia put together. The lantana attracts them. It was brought in from Europe as a garden plant, but in tropical conditions it runs wild. The margins of the rain-forest are smothered in it. Butterflies and lantana is a common sight up here. A brilliant Bird-wing a good eight inches across busily flapping its huge wings from flower to flower.'

It was no good pretending she wasn't fascinated. 'Would it be possible for me to take a close look at the rain-forest?' she asked him.

'I don't see why not. We could camp a day and a night there. It's a remarkable experience even in the mangrove forests, but I won't take you there. The mosquitoes would devour that white skin. The lagoons you will see. They're very beautiful, probably the most beautiful natural spectacles we've got.'

'Except for the crocodiles,' she said, and shuddered.

'The waterlilies usually cover them,' he said, and smiled. 'In any case, Katharine, the freshwater variety is fairly harmless and we won't put you in the way of the man-eaters. Only the foolhardy go

43

investigating beyond the water's edge. A few years ago a stockman of ours rode into a swamp. He lost a leg that way.'

Apprehension rippled over her. 'I hope we're not discussing what could possibly have happened to Darin.'

'No way.' He answered that emphatically, but how could he have known?

'Surely with your own stockman . . .' she persisted.

'Forget the crocodiles,' he said crisply. 'So many of them have been shot out they're even protected.'

'I can't forget anything,' she said, looking down at her hands. 'Death adders, tiger snakes . . .'

'Don't go into any more detail. Most of us manage to survive. It's all a question of where one puts down one's feet.'

Something inside her was beginning to hurt. She didn't belong here and Curt Dangerfield was doing his best to point that out. She couldn't bear his brilliant, green scrutiny, or the taunting note in his voice that was almost an insult. As it happened he didn't feel inclined to speak again until they were fast approaching the Half-Moon homestead, and its wide ring of satellite buildings.

Frowning, Katharine gazed down at the white jig-saw pattern flung down on the vivid green. It was admirable. Almost a country township. 'The Dangerfield empire. It's very imposing.'

He shrugged his own shoulders, catching the echo of her own mockery. 'You express yourself so beautifully.' He was suddenly aware he had hurt her. Was hurting her. 'Sorry, was that a hit?'

'It would be a disaster, wouldn't it, if we can't communicate at all?'

He brought his head back front again, his hand on the instrument panel. 'You're right, of course. You're fortunate indeed that I'm susceptible to blondes.'

'I can't think you're susceptible to any woman,' she said dryly.

'I'm no saint.'

'In that case, it might be best to avoid you.'

'Impossible. This is my world, Katharine Sutton. You came up here of your own free will. Now you take the consequences!'

They were descending and once again he had forgotten her, hands and mind intent on bringing the small plane down as smoothly as possible. The wheels touched down on the runway so gently that Katharine was unable to pinpoint the exact moment of contact. They were speeding towards a long silver hangar, then nearing it, Dangerfield brought the aircraft around, lightly touching the brakes. Another minute and the after-check was completed. Inside the hangar Katharine could see the yellow and white gleam of a bigger, much roomier plane, a twin-engined six- or seven-seater. Obviously she had come in economy class, though the sleek single-engined Cessna was supremely efficient.

Rather apprehensively she unbuckled her seat belt. The area was no longer deserted; people seemed to be coming from everywhere—stockmen in wide-brimmed dusty hats, their boots crunching, aboriginal women and children, a few piccaninnies in arms. Two white women joined them. Dangerfield turned to her and casually mentioned that she was under inspection. This brought Katharine's chin up. Her eyes sparkled and her hair danced and glinted in the bright bars of sunlight.

'Then we'd better get out and let them take a look.'

'That's my girl!' he said with something like admiration until she saw the green devilment in his eyes.

Mixed up with her feelings of anxiety and dread, her constant worry about Darin, was a weird, electric excitement, a feeling quite different from anything she had ever experienced before. Accustomed as she was to being honest with herself she was forced to admit it stemmed from Curt Dangerfield, the man on Malf-Moon. He went on ahead and lifted her out on to the hot tarmac. The welcoming party stood still for a moment, then they advanced. She couldn't run, so Katharine turned and threw up her head in the glittering sunlight, a movement that Dangerfield, the expert, associated with a highly strung filly. He was so close to her he could almost feel the nervous beat of her heart.

'Relax,' he said, and for the first time his voice was entirely kind, 'you're among friends!'

CHAPTER TWO

OVER dinner that evening, Katharine wasn't nearly so certain. There were four of them; Curt Danger-field, like a conqueror with an empire under his management, green eyes brilliant in his remarkable face; Viv Lake, his overseer, a blond giant of a man with a pleasantly dignified face; Martha Tyrrell, Curt's housekeeper-cum-co-ordinator, staff trainer and long-time friend, a sensible-looking woman in her fifties who extended friendliness and a great courtesy to all; and easily outshining her, Rada Lewis, Curt's widowed cousin, and very obviously Katharine's main problem.

All through the meal, Rada's slanting amber eyes moved constantly across Katharine's face, scrutiniz-ing her hard. There was something beyond a tem-peramental disparity in their yellow-gold blaze. Dark shadow beneath marked the eyes' curious glow-ing, staining the starkly white matt skin. A peony flame of colour lit the wide, narrow-lipped mouth spread over with a great dissatisfaction and the flat-tish bones of her face showed cleanly. Rada wasn't beautiful nor even pretty, but she was undoubtedly strikingly erotic, her jet-black hair worn short and dead straight with a full fringe showing plum high-lights. She was thin to the point of gauntness, yet she had a peculiar fluid elegance, a sinuousness, that reminded Katharine irresistibly of the undulating movements of a snake. She could have been the reincarnation of some pagan goddess; a diaphanous dark amber caftan glittered over her boneless limbs, around her neck a gold collar in the antique manner, each finger of her left hand dripping a different jewel. In Katharine's sheltered world, she was almost an unrecognisable type, but she had the sense to realise that such woman-thoughts were of little importance. Rada Lewis had endless fascination for men. She was a sorceress, very colourful and seething with passions, and her conquests had been many.

Her instant dislike and rejection of Katharine was like an actual scorching wave of heat on Katharine's face. She sat tense and distressed, toying with her wineglass, a beautifully prepared and presented main course virtually untouched. This decided Rada on the moment to strike, all previous conversation having been unburdened with worrying or anxious thought. She arched her long neck around, her voice from such an elegant body rather caustic to the ear, but the accent predictably polished:

'I can't imagine what you thought you'd gain, Miss Sutton, wandering about up here?'

This at least was very frank and revealing after all the masked stares. Katharine controlled her anger and irritation. 'I can't imagine why you should ask the question, Mrs Lewis. Darin is my brother.'

'I know that!' Rada hissed, her yellow eyes blazing, disgusted with Katharine's right to anything. 'But surely you know Curt is your only hope.'

Katharine's silver-grey eyes studied her host. 'I can take no one and nothing for granted,' she replied, low-voiced. 'Surely you can see I must do something myself? Darin is part of my life.'

'Then you're a very dedicated sister.' Rada shrugged her scorn. 'I never believed in them myself. The whole thing's too damned incredible!'

'You knew Darin?' Katharine challenged her, sweeping her blonde head up.

'Very slightly,' Rada conceded, frowning and unprepared for the attack on her sacred person. 'What I did know I didn't much like. Your brother seemed a very arrogant and conceited young man. He rather forced himself on me. No finesse!'

There was an instant reaction around the table. A gasp of protest from Martha, a tightening of the lips and a laid-down fork from Viv Lake, and for a moment a flash of censure from Curt Dangerfield. His low-toned order was as effective as a thundering shout.

'You can apologise for that, Rada. Katharine is our guest, and it's not in the least true in any case!'

'Oh God, Curt, you can be a brute! There's no need to pamper Miss Snowdrift. It *is* true, but you don't want to believe it.'

He lifted his head sharply, looking pretty formidable, and dutifully Rada addressed Katharine directly, a cruel amusement in her amber eyes.

'You *did* ask the question, Miss Sutton, but truly I didn't mean to offend you.'

'I can't forget it all the same. I assure you it doesn't sound in the least like Darin.'

'Do you think it possible a sister could judge?' Rada asked sweetly.

'I'd love to change the subject, wouldn't you?' Martha smiled at Katharine, sympathy in her hazel eyes. 'It's no secret that it doesn't pay to upset ourselves at dinner—leave that, dear, if you'd rather.'

Katharine shook her head very slightly. 'I'm sorry I can't do justice to such a beautiful meal. My travels seem to have caught up with me.'

'I know.' Martha's eyes swept over the girl approvingly. 'Curt tell me you're a teacher.'

'Marvellous! She can look after Sally!' Rada interjected with a half-savage abandon.

'And Sally is——?' Katharine looked from one to the other.

'Sarah. Rada's daughter,' Curt Dangerfield informed her.

'I've kept her in bed for a few days. She's had a bad dose of a virus,' Martha added. 'Sally is eight, going on nine. She's extremely intelligent!'

'And so *ugly*!' Rada moaned. 'Jeff's mother exactly!'

'I always thought Mrs Lewis a fine-looking woman myself!' Viv Lake said quite loudly, though it was obvious he found Rada as exciting as the next man.

'You're so unfailingly kind, Viv!' Rada turned the full battery of her eyes on him, causing the big man to flush slightly. 'Oh, I grant you the looks were agreeable in Jeff. A man can be unrelentingly ugly and still attractive, but a girl-child—I ask you! I've bent over backwards to do something about it, but now I think I'll just leave well alone.'

A great wave of compassion jerked the words out of Katharine. 'Poor Sally!'

'She plays the piano well,' Martha intervened hastily. 'I don't suppose you play yourself, Katharine?'

'Yes, I do,' Katharine said lightly, realising that Rada wasn't grateful to make the discovery. 'My mother was a great one for accomplishments and it was the done thing at the school I attended. I teach there now, as a matter of fact. I studied art and speech and ballet and a mixture of other things as well.'

'You were lucky!' Rada sneered. 'Darin had a different sort of tale to tell.'

'Let it go, Rada,' Curt said firmly, but the words hung in the air. For the first time Katharine realised that Rada's feelings for her cousin weren't exactly cousinly, and who could blame her? Curt Dangerfield was a man of exceptional charisma and Rada was smiling into his handsome face with the audacity and seduction of someone who was completely accepted—more, loved and admired. The gold collar, so beautifully wrought, glowed softly. It was a lovely thing, and seeing it Katharine sighed heavily, her sensitive face grave.

Martha across the table heard the sigh but was very careful not to take any notice. Rada was treating the girl's presence as an intrusion into her exclusive circle, but then Rada was cruel, a she-creature from a totally alien planet, full of duplicity and cunning. Martha disliked her intensely, but showed a tranquil face, after surviving one or two of Rada's emotional outbursts in the early days and her agility for placing the blame at Martha's feet. Curt had been drawn into it but refused to take sides. Rada needed calming and serious little Sally needed cheering. It was Martha's job to deflect Rada's sharp impatient temper from the child. In the six months Rada had been on Half-Moon, Martha had come to think of her as a kind of contamination. There was some evil enchantment about Rada. She fascinated every last man on the station, but she was worthless underneath. She had no veneration for anything or anybody, though she had been an obsession with Jeff. For all her sophistication and the experience she had amassed, Rada was a savage, with a molten glow to the depths of her eyes.

The newcomer, Katharine, was her absolute antithesis. Martha, finding her parallels in the world around her, thought of Katharine as Dawn; the pearly gleam of her skin, the pale stream of her hair, her silver-grey eyes. Rada suggested immediately the sudden furnace flames of sunset. Their looks could be the outward manifestations of the girls themselves. Katharine had a spiritual quality and a young dignity. Rada belonged in the wilds. Already Martha was hoping Katharine would have a purifying effect on the child. Rada should never have been a mother. She had no capacity for the role, though perhaps she might have been different had her child been a boy, eager and handsome.

Poor little Sally, for all her intelligence, obedient and no trouble, was rather desperately plain. She needed glasses and she had a stutter to boot. Rada often cast terrible glances at her and it was Martha's opinion that Sally was being severely damaged, perhaps irreparably, by her mother's rejection. There had been precious little joy in Sally's young life since her father had been killed demonstrating a high-powered sports car. Rada, more for spite than anything, had refused to allow the child to go to Grandma Lewis, whom she adored, so it was Curt who had come forward to invite the dry-eyed widow to recuperate on Half-Moon and bring with her the small bereft Sally. The gesture, to Martha's mind and that of the heartlessly treated Mildred Lewis, had been purely for the child's sake. Certainly Sally was happier and more enthusiastic since she had arrived, but her urgent need for love would never be fulfilled by her mother. What a terrible thing it was to create a feeling of humiliation in one's only child! Martha had even caught Sally with her broad, black-browed little face pressed up close to a mirror studying it. A little later Sally had pronounced herself: 'Agonisingly ugly!' The words and the intonation were Rada's exactly.

About this time hardworking and kindhearted Martha, the best housekeeper in the Far North, began to hate Rada with a violence that was unnatural to her. To hand out such punishment to a small child! Yet Sally had flashes of attractiveness when she was pleased or excited. Later on, perhaps, like her grandmother, she could develop her own special style. Viv Lake wasn't alone in thinking Mildred Lewis a fine-looking woman. She was famous for lots of things—her kindness and her hospitality, her way with the most hot-blooded horses, and she had the bearing of a duchess. Rada was the only one Martha could ever remember criticizing Mildred Lewis of River County.

It was Curt who broke the fraught little silence. 'If you can't eat anything, at least finish the wine,' he said, rather crisply, observing Katharine's extreme pallor. What little colour she had had seeped away, leaving her as pale as a china figure, her eyes no longer looking at him but through him—strange eyes, moonstones. She bothered him, an unfamiliar sensation. 'After that I think an early night.' He was plainly telling her, not suggesting. A man given to making decisions.

Rada clicked her tongue in unfeigned irritation. 'Don't pamper the girl. She may be a wee bit eccentric, but she's not a child!'

'Well, I think she looks like one,' he said with great calm. 'In fact, Katharine, I myself shall see you to your room.'

'That's funny!' snapped Rada.

'Perhaps. Coming, Katharine?'

Katharine jumped to her feet, her heart beating so rapidly she thought it would choke her. It would take a lot of practice to cope with Curt Dangerfield and his cousin. Martha and Viv Lake were on their feet too, staring at her with anxiety and a natural sympathy towards the stranger among them. Viv's long hands were thrust deep into his jacket pockets.

'I'm sorry we had to meet in such worrying circumstances, Miss Katharine, but we'll do everything we can to help you.'

'Thank you, Mr Lake.'

'Viv,' he supplied swiftly, throwing out a very attractive grin.

'Viv.' Her own face lightened. She was breathing a little easier now but loath to look back at Rada, like some yellow-eyed cobra just waiting to strike. Martha came part of the way, promising to look in later on with perhaps a nightcap.

Out in the hallway, Curt increased the gentle pressure on Katharine's narrow wrist. 'Stop shaking. You're not afraid of me?'

'My knees are trembling, but no, that would be too silly, wouldn't it?'

'Especially as we'll be seeing a good deal of each other. Here, come out into the night air for a few minutes. You're so white and tense you look as if you might pass out.'

'I won't,' she promised, yielding to his guiding arm. 'Whatever gave you that idea? I'm naturally pale.'

'Look.' He turned her round brusquely, making her face the huge hallway mirror with its decorated frame.

'I don't enjoy looking at myself these days.'

'I don't see why not! You're a very beautiful girl.'

'At least my appearance pleases you. Nothing else does.'

He drew her away from her own reflection. 'You should never have come here, Katharine, but now that you have, my home is your own.'

'I'm honoured to be in it, Mr Dangerfield.'

'Of course that deserves a slap.'

'I *mean* it. Half-Moon is very beautiful—the right setting for a very sophisticated man.'

'Who nevertheless works pretty hard for it. Try and remember that, will you, Katharine?' he said with the cool authority that was so much a part of him.

She averted her head, the light from the chandelier caught in her hair. She had drawn it away from her face and up at the nape, winding it into a silky coil, a style that seemed to emphasize her youth and her fairness. Tendrils brushed forward on to her cheeks and her eyes had captured a little of the delicate sage green of her dress. She would not look at him again, but he could see that her sensitive mouth was quivering.

'You're tearing yourself to pieces about Darin,' he charged her. 'There's not a shred of evidence that anything drastic has happened to him. He'll show up again.'

She swung up her head and encountered his probing, jade gaze. 'You say that as if you know!'

'Sad-eyes. Silver-eyes. I know Darin pretty well.'

'So do I.'

'I don't think so, little girl.'

The night was as fragrant as a gardenia, tropical, stirring the blood. In the darkness a cloud of perfume rose from the exotic banks of flowers, so persistent it disturbed the mind. Brilliant, over-size stars glittered in the dark purple sky and flurries of little iridescent insects haunted the vines. Half-Moon *was* very beautiful, a fitting symbol for the almost feudal authority Curt Dangerfield appeared to wield through a great beef empire. A primitive bark hut stood shadowy in the vast grounds, the first homestead of Philip Dangerfield, Curt's great-grandfather.

Katharine inhaled deeply, breathing the sweet, pure air. 'Your great-grandfather must have been a very brave man,' she said feelingly.

'My great-grandmother even more so!' He glanced at her sideways. 'How would you have reacted, I wonder, if you had been carried off into the jungle? You can imagine what it must have been like then.'

'Daunting. Dangerous?'

'Far worse than that. I'll let you read my great-grandmother's diary some time. It won't amuse you, though it shows indomitable humour. There's a portrait of her in the west wing. She looks every bit as sweet and fragile as you are.'

'I'm not fragile,' she protested.

'Perhaps not, but you sure give that impression, especially when you're asleep. Here, sit down.' Gently he pushed her back into a planter's chair and leaned negligently against the wrought iron balustrade facing her. 'Think of it, Katharine, hostility everywhere. Wild dogs, natives, snakes and crocodiles, sickness and swamp fever, a gently bred girl giving birth with only an old gin to help her. Incidentally, that same old gin saved the life of more than one Dangerfield according to the records. The plants of the rain-forest have remarkable medicinal properties and she must have known a great deal about them, though she never did part with one of her secrets. A member of her own family murdered three of our stockmen. They were camped on sacred ground, poor devils, and the myall went right out of his mind.'

Katharine pressed her head back against the canvas. 'This is an unfamiliar world. It almost belongs to the past.'

'Don't you believe it!'

'Then tell me more,' she invited.

'Are you interested?'

She turned her silver-gilt head along the chair,

moonlight running down her throat and slender body though his face was in darkness. 'You don't have to sound so sceptical. Of course I am.'

'Then I can do no less than oblige!' He swung away from the balustrade and hooked forward a chair, joining her to look out over the rustling garden. The stories he told weren't in the least bit soothing or gentle, yet Katharine lost all sense of time and tension, caught up as she was in the sheer and very personal drama of it all. These things had really happened, and they had all happened here on Half-Moon. His voice had an unusual, very attractive edge to it like steel under velvet. No wonder he had inherited a naturally autocratic style. It must have flowed from one generation to the other. It would take a strong man to keep these far-flung empires together. As he spoke she saw too why he had reacted so differently to Darin's disappearance. It happened a good deal up here. Men and women too became affected by the climate, by the colour and violence of the tropics. Katharine felt thousands and thousands of miles away from the life she had known, safety and familiar voices and scenes. Sensational things were day-to-day happenings on Half-Moon. A fruit-eating bat winged into the great mango trees, scattering the plump golden fruit. Katharine's eyes pinpointed its flight, a skeletal frame against the moon. She shivered in the flower-drenched night, the moon's radiance full on her face.

'That's it!' he announced with finality, as

59

though she were a child pleading for stories to keep her from bed. 'Come along, Katharine, the stars have fallen into your eyes.'

'Oh, I could listen to you for hours. Maybe for ever,' she said without thinking.

His strong hands reached for her so swiftly she almost fell backwards again. For the merest moment she was held close to him, which cost her all her serenity, a tingling sensation like a needle under the skin. Curt Dangerfield was very, very dangerous, and in the instant their eyes met he saw a very real apprehension.

'You're a strange girl,' he commented.

'Why? Tell me?'

He laughed and his teeth gleamed white. 'Maybe it's because you've done so little living, you're slow to know yourself.'

'I know I mustn't yield you an inch!'

'Why, Katharine!' he tipped his black head back, 'and I thought you so *quiet*!'

'Perhaps you crowd me. The wilderness is your territory, not mine.'

'It's no good pointing that out while you're here!'

Something about his voice, amused and mocking, the lazy-alert slant of his body, was evoking the strangest sensation, as sweet as it was savage. He said something in a language she couldn't understand and she looked up at him rather shyly.

'What was that?' she asked.

'Next year maybe I'll tell you.'

'What language was it?'

'A native dialect. Call it a night, Katharine, you look thoroughly distracted.'

'Curt——?' She was on the verge of telling him. She wanted to tell him, but he was Rada's cousin.

He caught hold of her hand, lightly, but it would have been impossible to break away. 'What is it? You've been trying to tell me something for most of the night.'

They had moved into the light of the hallway. It seemed shattering after the perfumed gloom. His brilliant green eyes were faintly hooded but trained on her. 'Well?'

She was just standing looking at him, like a snow maiden in the tropics, and his face hardened.

'So the moment's passed?'

'It was nothing. Just nothing.'

'I don't think that at all,' he said firmly. 'You were upset about something.'

'I just need my brother.'

'That's not what you need.'

For no reason she began trembling, so uncontrollably she knew she couldn't stand there talking to this man who appeared to have taken over her life. He shook her profoundly and she couldn't pretend he didn't. The dangerous words she had almost spoken she would keep to herself.

'So already you've learned to mistrust me?' he went on.

'It's not that at all. You sound almost bitter!'

'I'm allergic to that kind of thing. Don't try to keep things to yourself.'

'*You* do!' she hurled at him, her eyes great pools of light.

'All right. That's straightforward enough. Shall we agree to tell the truth to one another?'

'Good lord, I always tell the truth,' she answered automatically, almost swaying on her feet. 'The thing is, and you believe me already, we'll never see eye to eye on anything.'

'I told you not to come up here, but you couldn't curb your ...'

'... don't say *curiosity*,' she begged him, her soft voice cutting across his own.

'We can't discuss anything now,' he said, a little flatly. 'A good night's sleep might restore a little sanity.'

'To me?'

'Don't you think you could do with a good night's sleep?' he taunted her. 'In the morning it's up to you. Don't look at me as if I'm absolutely ruthless.'

She lowered her head to veil her opalescent eyes. 'I'm very grateful to you—far more than I'm saying. Perhaps I find your ... forcefulness a stumbling-block.'

His hard hand descended on her shoulder, turning her towards her room in the east wing. 'Have you forgotten the stories I told you already? It wouldn't do for a simple, good-natured soul to take over Half-Moon. You either. You have a legitimate cause for anxiety, but no cause for despair. You'll just have to trust me whether you want to or not. Put Darin out of your mind for the night. He'll turn up sooner or later with some story.'

'Darin could never be so irresponsible,' she declared.

'Couldn't he? I admire your loyalty, Katharine, but you're no shrewd judge of character.'

'Neither are you if you put him in charge of your outstation.'

'I didn't say he wasn't a good cattleman.'

'That's something!' she said with mock gratitude.

'It's not really fair,' he pointed out reasonably, 'to blame me.'

'Darin spoke of you in glowing terms. I'll never forget that.'

'The only mark in my favour? You must have a pretty grim opinion of me.'

They had almost reached the end of the gallery and he leaned forward and opened her door, glancing sideways at her pure, pale profile. 'I don't know why, Katharine, but you make me feel a hundred and fifty.'

So unexpected was his remark she turned and smiled at him, the laughter lighting her eyes and curving her lovely mouth. 'I've been very clumsy, haven't I? I'll gladly apologise.'

'The smile's enough,' he said almost abruptly, looking so vital and handsome that she laughed again.

'It's odd, but I'm on shifting ground with you,' she confessed.

'You haven't got the facts straight, Katharine— we're actually in the same boat. Sally, by the way, is in this wing.'

'Not with her mother?' she asked in astonishment.

'Sally picked out her own room,' he said dryly. 'It has a brass bed in it she very much admires.'

'Maybe I can look in on her,' Katharine suggested.

'If you like. She must be bored to distraction after a few days in bed. The sickness has passed off. It wasn't serious, but Martha wanted to be sure. Sally's a very nice little girl, and I don't want her to get hurt. Rada loves her, I'm sure, but unfortunately she doesn't seem able to express that love. Sally will be glad of the opportunity of having you around. Quite apart from your special training I can tell you could communicate with a youngster very easily. It's a gift, as I know I don't have to tell you. Rada doesn't have that gift, so in a sense Sally is a deprived child. It's evident anyway in her behaviour. I'll let you judge for yourself. One thing is certain, she has a superior brain. Encourage her, Katharine. You'll find she'll like you.'

'How long is she staying?' Katharine asked.

'That I don't know,' he said, his mood veering. 'They're welcome to stay as long as they like. I can't have a small girl's grief on my conscience. Nor a young woman's anxiety.' He swung about to stare at her, rather arrogantly Katharine thought, so that for a second she reacted automatically, her grey eyes blazing back into his own. A brass and glass lantern hung above her head, throwing into sharp relief the pearly pallor of her skin.

Curt clicked his tongue softly, derisively, then turned away to open out the dark-stained shuttered windows. 'It's time a properly brought up young woman was in bed.'

'I must admit I'm dead tired,' she said, her voice hushed in the huge, lovely room. 'It must suit you to hear it.'

'Why, exactly?'

'Well, goodness knows, so far you've managed to treat me like a child.'

'Well, Katharine, you've made the mistake of acting like one. I had rather a bad night last night myself.'

She flushed at his disturbingly hard expression, near shuddering at her own very distinct recollections. 'Barney stayed outside my door all night.'

'You needed him,' he pointed out crisply. 'Perhaps you'll understand now how important it is to do what you're told.'

'I'm sorry,' she said. 'It was terribly rash.' And it *was* rash, but did he have to look at her so lancingly? 'No one's ever spoken to me like this before.'

'Oh? Are there so many men in your life, then?'

His expression was baffling, though he held her gaze lightly. Too worldly. Too mocking. Despite the graceful indolence of his body, brilliantly alert.

He was not reassuring, vividly masculine in the beautiful but obviously feminine room. Defensively she sank into an old bentwood rocking chair, closing her hands over the polished curving sides. It began to tilt gently. 'This is marvellous,' she sidetracked, trying to gather her resources, but only succeeding in looking very young and vulnerable, her dawn-sky-coloured eyes enormous, half dazed with tiredness.

He stood looking down at her. 'Neatly evading the question! Yes, Katharine, that particular chair came out of Thonet's workshop. It's been in constant use ever since. It was a great favourite of my grandmother's. She was the one who started all the bush-houses you haven't seen yet. We've orchids from all over the world as well as our natives. They thrive in the open garden as well as the bush-houses. I continue to maintain them, seeing my grandmother went to great lengths to establish them. At one time she had agents collecting specimens from different parts of the world, South-East Asia and Brazil. You can see the results of their efforts tomorrow. Our orchids are famous.'

'You remember your grandmother well?' she asked.

'Of course I do. She lived until she was eighty-seven years old. I still *see* her, as a matter of fact, moving about the bush-houses—pure white hair and a soft white skin. She was an extraordinary woman. I adored her. She had grey eyes like you with lights in them depending on what colour she

66

wore—green or blue or violet. Moonstones, I suppose you'd call them. We never talked about my mother, her daughter. She died when I was five years old of swamp fever, and Gran reared me. She was a whole lot tougher than my father or grandfather, and they used to make strong men go pale.'

'That's not you, is it?' Katharine reached out for a photograph on the round table beside her. It was exceptionally good—a small boy about six or seven. Even at that age he was somebody, a very handsome little boy, with black curly hair and light shining eyes and a bright, audacious grin.

He shrugged lightly, by way of explanation. 'This was my grandmother's room.'

'Was it? Then I'm honoured. It's very beautiful.' She held the picture a moment longer, then put it down with a sigh. 'She must have escaped here.'

'Escaped?' he queried.

'From you men.'

'Oh!' He gave exactly the same grin. 'She never wanted to escape, young Katharine. In a way Gran created Half-Moon—not the holding, no woman could ever do that, but the homestead. No one ever disputed her here, not her superb taste nor her judgment. It was she who resolved on having the Dangerfield mansion in the wilds. You could set this house down on any estate in the world and it would hold its own.'

'I know. I'm all in favour of it, Mr Dangerfield.'

'Curt,' he corrected. 'With a C.'

'Katharine with a K,' she retorted dreamily,

turning her blonde head along the back of the chair. 'My friends call me Kat.'

'But how curious! It doesn't suit you at all. You're not in the least feline. Neither are you a Kate—but you're obviously falling asleep. Shall I ask Martha to help you?'

'No,' she said gently. 'I just might stay here and pretend I'm part of the past. I'll turn the light out and smell the gardenias and look out into the night. This is one of our historic homesteads, a frontier castle.'

'The mosquitoes will eat you alive. There's one posed along your shoulder.' He leaned forward and tapped his finger against the soft little hollow near her collarbone and a queer little pain slashed through her. 'The mosquitoes get up when everyone else has gone to bed. Pull your net, Katharine. That's an order.'

'I might suffocate,' she said, feeling she was suffocating then. Her heartbeats were shaking her. 'I hate nets.'

'*I'd* hate to see red weals on your skin, and they can become infected. No arguments, please, or I'll pull it myself.'

'I'll allow you to do that. It's perfectly plain I can't get up.'

'Really?' He was beside her, and she stared up at him breathlessly.

'From that I don't want you to gather I need a helping hand.'

'Be that as it may, you're getting one. I can well

68

see that a woman like you might need an escape route. My grandmother faced facts.'

'Damn your arrogance!' she said faintly, allowing herself to be half lifted to her feet. 'I can't feel you know me at all, Mr Dangerfield.'

'Ah, then why are you quivering?'

'I don't want to go any deeper.'

'I know you're intelligent, Katharine, but you haven't had a very extensive acquaintance with men.'

'They're not all that important in a girls' school.'

'That's not what my various nieces tell me. Everyone knows what girls think about most of the time.'

'They're improving,' she said. 'Pretty nearly all my students work hard. I can see that you're teasing me, but I can't see your motivation.'

Curt shook her slightly and she was forced to look up at him. 'Perhaps I'm trying to distract your mind. Services rendered, so you can get a good night's sleep.'

'You're very kind.'

'No, I'm not.'

'No, you're *not*! I spoke off the top of my head without thinking.'

'Naturally. Your eyes emphasize what you really believe.'

'Then I'd better proceed with extreme caution.'

'Exactly what I'd have said myself. Now I think my talents might extend so far as to pull that net.'

'I can do it, honestly.' She watched him move

away from her, his dark-timbred voice faintly laced with acid. She hadn't affronted him, but clearly she was annoying him with the minimum of effort.

'Here, catch!' He hurled a pillow at her and for a miracle she caught it, hugging it to her slender frame like some kind of armour. This started him laughing and the moment of antagonism passed

'I begin to ask myself why you're being nice to me?' she queried.

'I always do my level best for damsels in distress, Miss Katharine. Now,' he looked around the room quickly, then back to her, 'I think you can manage the rest. I want you to promise me one thing.'

'I'll do *my* level best.'

'You'll take every last piece of advice I give you from now on.'

'Well ...' she hesitated.

'It's safer. Anyway, shelve the matter until the morning. At which time you might tell me what you were going to tell me before.'

Irresistibly her eyes travelled over his face. Handsome as it undoubtedly was, it was rather a relentless face, green eyes narrowing, a challenging angle to his decisively cleft chin. Something urged her to tell him, and at once, but the words refused to form themselves in her mouth, at least in a way he might find acceptable.

'Well then ...' He was obviously maddened by her curious reverie, though he was studying her every bit as intently as she was studying him. 'I'll say goodnight. You could, if you chose, Katharine, drive me mad.'

'Not as bad as that, surely?'

His gaze was so very clear it was almost green ice. 'For no other reason than you're a good half dozen years on the charming and helpless side. Old habits die hard.'

'I don't follow you at all.'

'Mercifully!' he said dryly.

There was a fraught silence while Katharine continued to stare at him, compulsively, her eyes shimmering. It didn't seem possible, but she didn't want him to go. He was so vivid, so *immediate*, there was a whole world of profit in his presence alone. It didn't seem possible either, but he was no stranger to her. She had known him before, in another life. Then, as now, her feelings for him had been not unmixed with a curious trepidation.

Curt seemed to share her preoccupation, his eyes lit with an ironic amusement. 'I have the idea, Katharine, I've met you some time before.'

'You're troubling me, too,' she said, her voice faintly melancholy. 'I suppose it's really a subject for a psychologist.'

He smiled at that, the skin stretched taut against the bold modelling of his cheekbones. 'I don't need any help, Katharine, though it's apparent someone has to protect you from yourself.'

'Surely that's your idea of a cruel joke?'

'Who's cruel?' he asked her, his green eyes probing her face, searching deep into her heart and her brain.

'Isn't a cleft chin a sign of ruthlessness?'

'Is it?' He reached out and clasped her wrist, his fingers an iron bracelet. 'Even if it was, which I seriously doubt, I wouldn't let it worry you. You're just a bad case of the jitters, a sad little girl in a strange land.'

'As far as I'm concerned I'm quite grown up,' she insisted.

'We won't argue to what degree. To me, you look desperately young.' For an instant his face wore a remote brooding look that startled her.

'Come back,' she said, as much for him as for herself.

'Is that a plea? Your voice makes me believe it.'

'I expect it's because you looked very sombre.'

'At least you recognised it,' he said. 'That's something, isn't it?'

His tone nettled her. 'If it's true, why? I know what you represent up here, but you must let me know what steps you will take.'

'*Taken*, don't you mean? The trouble with Darin is, he can't do a good job without complications.'

Startled and angry, she looked up at him. 'What proof have you got that he's still alive? You sound so sure of yourself.'

'My dear little girl,' he said bluntly, 'I can obtain information from all sorts of channels, official and otherwise.'

'An efficient espionage system.' His manner drove her on.

'Don't sound so biting. It doesn't suit you.'

'A true statement, surely?' she persisted.

'It sounds a bit like it, I must admit. Let go of this dedicated air, Katharine, for your own sake. I wanted you to keep out of it.'

'That I cannot possibly do.' She turned her head away, the soft brilliancy of the chandelier emphasizing her look of shining delicacy.

Curt's own expression seemed to harden. 'No.' he agreed with finality. 'You've committed yourself pretty fully. Let me say only, it's safer and wiser to leave the whole business to me.'

'There's no danger, is there?' She looked back at him, her grave eyes measuring his face.

For a split second he seemed to hesitate, then he shrugged his wide shoulders as though tiring of the whole thing. 'I can do a lot of things, Katharine, you can't.'

'So I just have to depend on you?'

'Is that so bad? You could look a little happier about it.'

'This isn't a pleasure trip, Mr. Dangerfield.'

'*Curt*,' he suggested rather crisply. 'Call me Curt.' His green eyes were brilliant, faintly angry, as befitting the absolute monarch of his own world.

'Curt by name, curt by nature,' she offered patly.

'As a matter of fact, I'm anything but that. A lot of people find me perfectly pleasant. I'm interested in peace, not war. Sociable experiments like this

73

one!' His right hand moved out and twisted her head up, stroking the blonde hair back from her face. 'You and Darin do have a certain family resemblance,' he said slowly, 'both of you seem bent on sabotage.'

'That isn't true,' she said, almost closing her eyes against him. 'It just isn't true.'

'No?'

The room was rocking round him, rising and falling, so that for a moment she thought she would faint. Some dark aura was on him, a kind of hard recklessness he had been fighting all day.

'You're hurting me!' she said, though his fingers were barely bruising her skin.

'I'm sorry.' Immediately his hold lightened, but still lingered. 'Such a soulful little victim, when you've not the faintest notion just how chivalrous I'm being. Remember, Katharine, you've upset all my meticulous plans!'

Her fine, white-petalled skin seemed on fire. She was standing so close to him she was almost afraid of herself. Never had she experienced desire nor even understood it, but now she knew what it could do. 'This can't be happening!' she said, nearly lost in sensation.

'Why not? Emotions blossom in the tropics. It's pretty hectic up here—something to do with the heat and the rain-storms. Consider the lilies on the lotus ponds, Katharine.' His green eyes swept her face, a deliberate challenge that made her flash out at him:

'Stop! Don't dare try to colour my judgment!'

'Which only goes to incite me further. Such a dangerous indulgence, daring me. The last straw!'

Katharine threw up her head, trying to measure up to him, but the mockery in his eyes only deepened. He caught her against him almost leisurely, bent his head, touched her mouth lightly, with such a smooth arrogance and pleasure she yielded dizzily against him, too outmanoeuvred to resist. It would have been hopeless anyway. There was an odd pitch of intensity to all this, a glitter of hostility, a powerful sexual spark. When he finally released her, she still had to lean against him, which made it all the more humiliating. 'That was unforgivable!'

Unexpectedly he laughed. 'Keep all the complaints for the morning. That should be an activity in itself. You're rather a puzzle, Miss Gossamer Eyes. You look as cool as a gardenia, but just then all the coolness cut out.'

Katharine had no answer to that. She wanted to retaliate, but she was ashamed of her own reactions, like a bonfire within her. Never had she considered emotional involvement, but here it was close at hand. A man so forceful could rule one's entire life.

'Nothing's real,' she said plaintively.

'I thought we made perfectly clear that it is. Now, I'm making a serious bid to go. You're not frightened of thunderstorms as well?'

She would have liked to make a rush at him to

stop him, but she had already made a fool of herself. She sank into the rocking chair, trying to speak lightly. 'I'm not overly enthusiastic about either, but in that big, beautiful bed I just might fall into a magic sleep.'

'I rather fancy you might. There's no point in looking a dream if you can't act it out.'

'I gather you don't approve.'

'I don't know,' he drawled lazily. 'You're very interesting in a fey sort of way. I just wanted to warn you of a possible thunderstorm. It's the usual thing this time of year.'

'Another sort of warning might have been more pertinent. Do you always kiss your house guests goodnight?'

'Actually almost never. It takes a very special kind of girl to arouse me.'

His dark masculinity was almost frightening in such a feminine room. 'Surely you don't think it was a mutual passion?' she asked faintly.

'I'd say so,' he stressed briefly. 'Now this is hardly the time for melodrama. I think Martha mentioned to you that she'll be bringing you a nightcap?'

'I don't really need anything,' she said, feeling just as unstrung as she could have been.

'I think you do.' His green gaze whipped over her, lingering on the pulse in her throat. 'We Dangerfields have a passion for running people's lives. Isn't that what your innocent imagination has been telling you?'

'Yes.'

His ironic little laugh was like a velvet bell in his throat. '*Goodnight*, Katharine.'

'Goodnight, Mr Dangerfield. I realise now I really know absolutely nothing about you.'

'Well, I know a lot about you. Perhaps fortunately.'

She let her head droop into her hand, exposing her creamy, vulnerable nape. All that splendid dark insolence was too much for her, yet he was looking at her with coldly amused detachment. 'I might have done better staying at home.'

'Instead of which you've set yourself up as a sacrificial lamb. So be it!'

After he had gone, Katharine looked around the room with some bewilderment. In a few short hours, Curt Dangerfield had become a force in her life. How had it happened, and so easily, almost inevitably? Even in kissing her he had secured a psychological advantage, both curious and frightening. A man of infinite calculation, perhaps he had kissed her for just that reason. There had been a recharging tension between them all day, and the kiss had confirmed it. Now it seemed to her that she had undergone some startling change.

She turned her head, examining her face in the Victorian swing mirror. It still looked the same. It wasn't her first kiss, assuredly, but now it dawned on her that up until a few minutes ago she hadn't known the first thing about it. Curt Dangerfield was a man of experience and considerable skill, and thinking this, she stiffened, almost fanatical about her personal dignity. She was known to be, and was, a very fastidious girl, yet here she was rocking herself back and forth as though she harboured a secret passion.

Still, it was difficult to calm down after a kiss like that. Her mouth still quivered and the male scent of him clung to her. Above all, she was forced into realising just how vulnerable she had been made to become. It was in Curt Dangerfield's power to hurt her. She hadn't rocked herself this madly since she was ten years old on her grandmother's veranda. Obviously such a sensuous and reckless clash could never be allowed to happen again, for being with Curt Dangerfield was like being swept along on a wild current, and now he was gone, she felt stranded on the oceans of carpet. She had to think about anything but this man on Half-Moon. His effect on her was her second major shock when her anxiety for Darin was bad enough. If he were alive, surely he would contact her soon.

In the open doorway Rada Lewis suddenly materialised, staring with some fixity at the girl in the rocking chair. 'If you're supposedly so tired,' she burst out explosively, 'why don't you go to bed? You look ridiculous sitting there, like a stunned rabbit.'

Katharine, unaware of her until she spoke, started to get up. 'Oh well,' she said lightly, determined not to let Rada upset her, 'I suppose I might as well. At least I'm not drunk!'

Rada had certainly done better than average at dinner, but the little tilt in no way went home. She swung the door shut behind her and advanced on Katharine as though she was about to teach the younger woman a lesson, employing a very strong tone: 'You know something? This is no time for reticence. It was all your own idea coming up here, now there's no use crying about it, like some little idiot out of the movies. I want you to promise me one thing—in fact, I absolutely *insist.*'

'Do tell me,' Katharine invited, fascinated and repelled by Rada's massive arrogance.

'Get out of here,' Rada exclaimed bitterly, 'just as quick as you can. If you don't you might live to regret it.'

'You're looking at a survivor,' Katharine said calmly. 'What did you think I was—a rag doll?'

'No. You're just making the mistake of your life.'

'What, making enquiries about my brother?'

'I think Curt pledged himself to do that, but why he should bother...' Rada broke off with a contemptuous wave of her hand.

'Wouldn't you go after someone who was lost?' Katharine queried.

'*Lost*? Have you gone raving mad?'

Katharine found herself trembling. She put her hands to her hair and loosened the silky coil until it fell in a soft, shining curtain round her shoulders. 'I keep waiting for a climax,' she said painfully.

'Someone to actually *tell* me something, not petrify me with wild statements. As far as my going is concerned, surely Mr Dangerfield has all the say?'

'*Curt*,' Rada explained with the utmost icy precision, 'has vouchsafed me this little job. Naturally he didn't want to deliver any ultimatums himself!'

'Which is all very well for your story, but it's simply not true! What little I've seen of Mr Dangerfield he would scarcely need to hide behind your skirts. The idea is ludicrous. I'm sure his nerve is demonic and what you're saying is weak. It's not the name of the game, and he's not the man for the part.'

'You think I'm a liar?' Rada hurled at her, her eyes glittering in her flushed face.

'On this particular subject, *yes*,' Katharine said bravely, for violent temper was disfiguring Rada's face. 'I realise you don't like me.' *An understatement*. 'I know you don't want me here, but I'm afraid I'll have to ignore your warnings. You see, it's Darin I'm interested in, after all.'

'How dare you!' Rada said ringingly, an uncanny wildness about her. 'I'm not here as some sort of rival!'

'I didn't precipitate this scene, Mrs Lewis, *you* did. May I remind you I'm not stone? If you insist on attacking me, surely I'm allowed a few thrusts. It seems only fair.'

Rada slid forward in slow motion, a weirdly dominating figure, and despite herself Katharine found herself backing. 'Indeed you are,' Rada agreed with soft menace, 'it's just that you're getting yourself into really hot water. What do you know of your precious brother beyond all the silly, innocent kid stuff?'

'I know he was foolish enough to fall in love with you.'

'*He*? How could he?'

As a weapon it was a piece of inspired brilliance, for Rada had come to a full stop, her face whitening to a pitiable degree. Now that she had said it, Katharine had no option but to continue with such a formidable subject. 'He *did*,' she said quietly.

Rada's confidence that appeared to have run out suddenly took on an entirely fresh impetus. 'A stockman, an employee, to look so high?'

'For all your elegance and glamour I think you're appalling.'

Rada walked briskly to the window and looked out of it. 'Your opinion is entirely irrelevant!' She seemed quite sure of herself and her colour was returning. 'How contemptible of you to suggest that I would even look sideways at your brother.'

'You mightn't strike everyone as all that splendid,' Katharine said clearly.

'You cheeky little bitch!'

'Never. I'd only be an amateur beside you. It all ties in pretty strongly with your image. A woman like you could probably turn Darin into a madman —temporarily, one hopes!'

'How clever of you!' Rada laughed, prepared to accept that she could do just that.

'It proves my point, if it needed proving, that is,' Katharine said hardily.

'You might tell me what you're getting at,' said Rada, beginning to get worked up again. 'It's war between us.'

'I don't really care, though I realise you're probably fantastic at that sort of thing!'

'The wicked temptress!' Rada shrilled, her wild eyes betraying her. 'Your brother isn't the only imbecile in your family.'

'Let's clear that point up! My mother, for instance, would never have parted with that gold collar you're wearing. You would know, of course, that it's valuable?'

Rada's matt white skin was distinctly dewed with sweat, all the blustering arrogance retreating. 'I don't know what you're talking about.'

'You do. In my own view it was imbecilic of you to wear it. Darin gave it to you, didn't he?'

'I think not!' Rada said violently, an ugly anger vying with the extent of her own involvement.

'Take it off. Show it to me,' Katharine invited. 'There are linked initials on the clasp.'

'I certainly don't have to do that!' Rada protested as though the suggestion was preposterous. 'The ownership of this collar is very much my own affair. It's a beautiful piece of work, but I don't imagine it's a one of a kind. Your mother may well have owned a similar piece.'

'It belonged to my grandmather, actually,' Katharine said calmly. 'I have a locket of hers over there on the bureau. Inside the locket is a photograph of her as a young bride. She was wearing it then—a present from my grandfather made up to his own design. Would you care to see it?'

'I don't. In fact, if there are two of them, I don't want this one at all!' Rada ripped the gold collar from her and hurled it to the floor.

Katharine retrieved it, holding it tenderly. 'There were no initials, but of course Darin gave it to you, and we both know why.'

'In which case,' Rada lashed back spitefully, 'Darin is a thief! He would *do* anything, be *in* anything, to get money! You'd better pray Curt doesn't catch up with him, otherwise our Darin might wind up in jail!'

'You're the only one who has implied that!'

'My dear! Work it out for yourself. Your brother is an adventurer, a ne'er-do-well. Are you completely stupid, or must I draw pictures?'

'Only yours is necessary. It explains a great deal. If Darin gave you this, he must care deeply for you. He had enough family feeling left.'

'You over-emphasize your point, little girl!' Rada sneered maliciously. 'Certainly I'm not averse to a man's admiration, but let's look at the facts. A man simply must provide an excellent living, and Darin wasn't going anywhere. Isn't that so? A manager of an outstation!'

'It was a start!'

'I wouldn't look at less than a millionaire!' Rada

stated emphatically, feeling herself quite rightly pressed to the limit.

'Then your cousin seems to qualify,' Katharine returned coolly.

'Assuredly!' For an instant Rada's red rage seemed to blaze at her. 'And just as assuredly, it's none of your business. I've already found what *I* want. I'd advise you to move on before something unpleasant overtakes you.'

'I'll go when I'm convinced Darin is in no danger.'

'How blind can you get?' Rada almost shrieked at her. 'How much do you earn as a schoolteacher?'

'Enough,' Katharine said with complete surprise.

'All right!' Rada slapped one bejewelled hand into the other. 'I'll pay you to go away again.'

'But how extraordinary!'

'You accept?'

'Don't think of it!' Katharine said rapidly. 'Surely you're betraying yourself somehow? Why on earth would you pay me to go away again? It doesn't make sense unless you know something you're not saying.'

'Darin made a run for it,' Rada announced abruptly, looking straight ahead of her as though her control might fail her. The sinister influence behind her exotic sophistication was never more in evidence. 'You don't mean anything to your brother, but you might fall a casualty to his little game.'

'In which you would seem to be implicated!'

'*Please!*' Rada threw up a scornful hand. 'Darin's a quick worker, but his decisions of late have been less than brilliant. By the time Curt has got through with him . . .'

'Where *is* he?' Katharine interrupted.

'How should I know?' Rada flashed her an odd glance, part arrogance, part crumpled hate.

'You more than anyone,' Katharine returned quietly.

'I know nothing!' Rada insisted explosively. 'It's been like some frightful nightmare for all of us.'

'I don't follow.'

'Is it necessary you should? All you have to do is obey me. Go back where you belong. Darin may be your brother, but to you he's a closed book. Depend on him and you'll be bitterly disappointed.'

'I think I can promise you I only want to make sure he's alive,' Katharine assured her.

'Well, don't use this roof as some kind of protection. Darin's alive. He just has to change his tactics. You know he was involved in the illegal trafficking of birds?' Rada gave the younger girl an indifferent glance that brightened with malice. 'Oh dear, a sour note, when I thought you knew. Yes, apparently he felt he could steal what he liked.'

'Darin wouldn't do anything so miserable,' said Katharine, though she was beginning to visualise his doing just that.

'Come off it!' Rada laughed scathingly. 'Don't look as if I've ruined your young life. Hustling birds wouldn't disturb Darin. They fetch a fine price in Hong Kong, especially the Golden Throat.'

'And you're telling me he was actually convicted of this?'

'Not convicted, no. He and the birds conveniently disappeared. There have been stock losses as well.'

It occurred to Katharine, as pale as alabaster, that the room was beginning to spin. 'Why didn't Mr Dangerfield tell me?'

'Perhaps he realised such a touching little-girl faith would be hard to shed. Curt picks his targets and you look a mere child sitting there, even a little retarded. I'm sorry to have to do this, but Darin's behaviour has been utterly contemptible. If you're wise, you'll please go away.'

'There must be something in it for you. What?'

Rada's narrow golden eyes dilated. 'I owe you no answers. In fact, I'm indifferent to your plight, whatever that might be. You've made a trip up here for nothing. Curt's done everything he could on your behalf and it seems to me he's letting you down pretty lightly. What Darin is involved in isn't pretty. It was bound to come sooner or later—any scheme at all to bring in some ready money.'

'And for you!' Katharine struck home, her grey eyes intent.

Rada whirled about, her eyes full of fire, but the shock was still showing. 'Don't say that again!' she exclaimed in an intimidating manner.

'Why not? You're the woman. I knew there was one.'

'You imagine I got my hooks into him?'

'I didn't say it. The gold collar told me. Probably you were the most important thing that had ever happened to him. The Arabian Nights, the Queen of Sheba, at any rate a professional Circe.'

Rada's hand shot out and connected, an expert hard slap. 'You're the most stupid creature imaginable! I hardly gave a thought to him. Don't blame me if your brother got mixed up in all the old rackets.'

'And who brought him into them? *You?*' Katharine put up a hand to her smarting face, but otherwise was seemingly untouched.

'Are you threatening me?' Rada's voice rose sharply, her eyes brilliant with sudden, intense emotion.

'Why does the aggressor always say that? Tell me, Mrs Lewis, where do you get your information from?'

'Don't worry about that!' Rada answered promptly. 'I deal with the facts, despicable as they seem to be. Nevertheless, I'm still capable of suggesting it's suicide for you to remain up here.'

'How theatrical! Even if it were true, I don't care about that now. I'm staying—and by the way I think you're pretty appalling. Glittery, but still a fishwife.'

'And I'd like to break your silly little neck with one blow,' Rada responded, staring at Katharine intently as though she was considering how best to go about it.

Despite herself Katharine laughed. 'I know the type. How lucky you are I'm not at all violent. It's inexcusable in a woman, almost a crime.'

'Don't you look so smug about it. No doubt your dear brother will go to jail. At least I hope so. Not what you expected, is it, dear? If you'd tried to be co-operative, I might have helped you.'

'No doubt we'll come to your reasons,' Katharine said dryly.

'Meaning what?'

'There's an explanation for your behaviour,' Katharine said finally.

There was a short rap at the door and they both stared at it blankly, hardly daring to breathe. A second later it opened and Martha Tyrrell came into the room, looking searchingly from one to the other, seeing the odd look of fright in Rada's eyes abating. It wasn't Rada, however, who concerned her, but their young visitor.

'I wouldn't stand about talking if I were you, Katharine,' she said. 'You look about ready to drop.'

'And I'm the one who's been keeping her awake!' Rada said gaily. 'Okay, I'll see myself out. Sleep well, Katharine, and remember what I told you. It was all gold.'

'What's wrong?' Martha asked abruptly, after Rada had gone.

'It looks bad for Darin, doesn't it?' Katharine managed, equally terse.

'What's Rada been telling you?' asked Martha.

'Possibly the truth.'

'Which is?'

'Darin hasn't passed up one opportunity for making easy money.'

'Rada always did like slinging mud about. One day she won't miss it. Maybe she was the motive.'

Katharine sat down hard on the bed. 'I challenged her with that and received a thundering retort. But he has, hasn't he?' she asked sadly.

'I don't know what Rada told you.'

'Birds. Cattle.' Katharine said with false calm.

'Birds, yes,' Martha burst out unhappily. 'He's not the first to come at that. Some even boast about it—a lucrative sideline. About the cattle I can't say. On a station this size it's impossible to patrol the whole Run. We've had stock losses, certainly. Whoever is responsible, they're pretty highly organised, but Curt doesn't know or isn't saying whether Darin was mixed up in it. There have been leakages of information as well. Confidential Dangerfield transactions, property sales, that kind of thing.'

'Surely Darin wouldn't have access to that?'

'For a while there, Curt really trusted him,' Martha said heavily, 'He gave him a promotion and the opportunity to improve himself. Half-Moon isn't the only Dangerfield station. The properties link up through the Centre down to the Channel Country. Darin, if he had proved himself, could have found himself manager of any one of them. I could have sworn that was just what he wanted. All he had to do was show he was competent and one hundred per cent reliable.'

'And he didn't do that?'

'No, I'm sorry, my dear, he didn't. I liked him. It's my opinion he fell hook, line and sinker for Rada, but he would never have made it with her. A little excitement, that's all. Rada is accustomed to admiration, and I feel I must warn you she's dangerous. She won't scruple to put you in the wrong, that's been brought home to me at high speed. I'm only saying this because I can see she's chilled you through to the bone.'

'Or put me through a shredder! It all fits, but I can't take it in.'

Martha started back to the door and turned to speak to her. 'I guess we can all get through this, Katharine. You want the true picture. Stay. I'll be very glad of your company and so will young Sally. Don't let Rada wipe you out.'

'What about Mr Dangerfield?' Katharine lifted her head.

'Curt is someone to hold on to through a cyclone,' Martha said wryly. 'The only time you need worry is when he shows you the door.'

'He didn't want me here.'

'Now it's the other way round,' Martha said plainly. 'I think you'll find he'll insist on your staying on, at least for a little while. Don't worry, my dear, Curt's absolutely super, a very special person. It's not unusual with the Dangerfields. I worshipped the ground his grandmother walked upon—we all did. Don't take Rada as typical of the family,' she went on. 'She's not typical at all. I've never met another one like her. There are things about her only another woman sees. In the days ahead, don't fly to Sally's defence. It will only rebound on the child. You'll see the situation as you go along. None of us bother Curt with questions, we just wait on him. I'd advise you to do that. You'll find he's on your side.'

'Yes,' Katharine agreed quietly, 'but it would be an impossible task if he's gunning for Darin.'

Martha visibly sighed. 'I can only say again, if there's any mess to clear up, let Curt handle it. He knows best. He's been trained to take over the reins since he was a small boy. He's in touch with all the authorities and he can pull any number of strings. If Darin deserves some kind of punishment, and I sincerely hope he doesn't, you can hope for justice with a strong dash of mercy. Curt is a very generous man, though I wouldn't care to cross him myself.'

'It's as simple as that, then!' said Katharine. 'Hard and strong and clever. He doesn't push it, I have to admit. It's all there.'

'Have courage, child!' Martha smiled at her.

'Maybe tomorrow. Thank you for being so kind to me, Mrs Tyrrell.'

'*Martha*,' the housekeeper invited. 'I'm Martha to everyone around here. Drink up that milk—it's laced with something extra. Sleep easy, my dear. Things always look better in daylight.' She went ahead and pulled the door after her, flashing a smile as she went.

Katharine took a grip on herself and began to sip the hot milk. Something extra wouldn't change anything, but it might get her through the night. Some good had to come out of all this, but she could never go to Rada Lewis for a character reference. It had its funny side, but Rada hated the sight of her. Why?

CHAPTER THREE

For a few hours more night slumbered in a humid hiatus that made even a cool top sheet unbearable, then shortly after midnight, the storm broke in fury. Great rounds of thunder shattered the silence and in its wake, lightning, showering Katharine's room in a radiant white light. She woke in confusion, murmuring over and over: 'Oh no!'

Outside the garden was moaning and a bird shrieked as though shot. It sounded to Katharine, so recently deeply asleep, quite shocking. So this was the end of the Dry! It was utterly elemental, the explosive clap of the thunder, a sky that ran with a liquid white fire. Another flash revealed the sheer curtains whipping about crazily like ghosts. At a rush, before the rain fell, Katharine pushed back the netting and padded across the room to the French doors.

Beyond the encircling verandah, the great ornamental trees of the garden, the scarlet blossoming poincianas, were being lashed about in a fury. The rain came a few seconds after, a prolific deluge under which the whole world seemed to drown. It even seemed possible that the house, that had been built to withstand cyclones, might be swept away. Katharine stood there in her thin nightdress stilled into fascination. Every living thing just had to be awake. No one could sleep through such a massive bombardment, that made even her ears ache. As an example of her first tropical thunderstorm she would remember it. She was still immersed in the savage flickering of the lightning when a young, very unsteady voice spoke behind her.

'Who's that?'

Katharine wheeled around, almost incapable of answering for a moment until she made out the small figure that had emerged like a frightened bird from the adjoining bedroom. 'You're Sally.'

'Yes, I am.' The voice was quivering badly.

Katharine put out a reassuring hand, changing automatically to her schoolteacher voice, superb for calming small children. 'I'm Katharine,' she said conversationally, as though it was the middle of a blue summer's day and not a shattering rainstorm that flowed all over them. 'I've come to join you for a while. Come over by me. I'm not surprised you can't sleep.'

Sally's small figure swayed whitely, then a clammy little hand accepted Katharine's own and held there. 'Yes, it's awful, isn't it?' she volunteered, and Katharine could see she was close to real terror. 'I can't get used to these storms. They're so loud and the trees go bang against the walls. I'm sure one of them will topple down on us.'

'I shouldn't think so,' Katharine said, before the fury of the storm. It had been her own fear as well. 'They must be immensely strong. Why, they've been challenging the elements for a hundred years. This is my first experience of a great thunderstorm. You must be a few up on me. It's very spectacular—rather like a wicked, mad fairy with a magic wand. Look over there!'

Sally had never thought of it as a game. She absorbed the sight of the dancing dangerous lightning in silence, then snatched a breath. 'The rain is *so* melancholy. It makes me cry, the way all the leaves drip down. Sodden.'

'Witches wailing?' Katharine suggested.

'You're funny!' smiled the child.

'Let's think of the trees as castles. The great branches are the turrets. No matter how loud the thunder, how vivid the lightning, they won't know fear. Haven't you a favourite tree?'

'Not here. Here the wind tears at the leaves and the fruit bats get in the mangoes. You should hear them shriek! They gorge themselves on the hanging fruit. The trees here are too big. They spread everywhere.'

Such a desolate little girl she sounded. Katharine put a protective arm around the thin shoulders. 'What about going back to bed?'

'Lightning is dangerous,' Sally maintained, staring out at it fixedly.

'So bright and untamed. Would you like me to close the shutters?'

'Then I'd suffocate.'

'Well, you'd better come in with me. See, the air's much fresher now. It will be over soon, I'm sure.'

'Well, it's frightened me breathless. There's no magic for me.'

'You have to look for it, Sally.'

'May I look from your room?' the child asked.

'Certainly. The bed's big enough for a dozen small friends.'

Inside the bedroom, Katharine switched on a light and felt a sharp sense of dismay at Sally's pathetic little face. She was small for her age, at the moment rather distressingly plain, freckles standing out very clearly, brown eyes unnaturally bright. Tendrils of hair escaped her thin little plaits when she really needed a full fringe and a short blunt cut.

'Don't be afraid, Sally,' Katharine said quietly.

'I'm not afraid now.'

'Surely it wasn't just the thunderstorm?'

'Oh, being on my own, mostly, I suppose. Anyway, I'm better now. Thanks for coming to my rescue. You're even prettier in the light.'

'What a nice thing to say!'

'But it's true. Look at me!' Sally suddenly spun about and faced the cheval-glass.

'I'm looking, and I like what I see,' Katharine said promptly. 'Your freckles are standing out and you're very white. That's from trying not to cry.'

'My mother says I'm ugly.' Sally crumpled and there was shame in her face.

'Mothers sometimes say things they don't mean,' Katharine said soothingly.

'Oh no, she means it.'

'I expect in a few years, Sally, you'll look very distinguished,' Katharine offered, anxious to wipe away Rada's insult.

'I'd rather look like you,' said Sally. 'Even your hair would do. What a fabulous colour! It doesn't matter that it's straight.'

'Into bed with you, Sally. You're still just a baby. There's plenty of time for you to go into the beauty business. Which side do you want?'

'The one nearest the bureau.'

'Right, then, hop in. Tomorrow we have lots to do, you know.'

Sally's small squarish face suddenly blossomed and her brown eyes grew absorbed. 'Oh, really? What?'

Katharine regarded her for a moment. 'I'll leave that to you. You must know all the best beauty spots.'

'Oh, I do!'

Sally was smiling and it gave Katharine great satisfaction. Sally smiling was a changed person. As a smile it could hardly have been bettered, as though her repressed spirit was suddenly freed. The thunder now was muffled with only an occasional zigzag of forked lightning. Katharine turned out the light and sank on to the bed. 'I'll be very glad of your company, Sally.'

'Oh, really? Thank you,' Sally said sleepily, and fell into a child's instant deep sleep, her head buried like an ostrich half under the pillow.

Katharine smiled to herself as her own head started to droop. What a heartbreaking child!

Lonely, unloved by her own mother. Rada would have no patience with a plain, rather timid little girl. Rada was amazingly arrogant. The rain continued to come down in a soaking roar, but soon Katharine too was fast asleep with Sally's warm little body hard at her back. They were the innocents. Rada was the pagan.

The birds woke her; lorikeets in a nectar-induced ecstasy in the banksia trees. It wasn't quite seven. Beside her, bunched up in the sheets, Sally was gently dreaming of the long trek before them, judging from her expression. It stirred Katharine's heart. She bunched her own pillow by the child's side and got up. She felt well and rested and the sight and the sound of the birds was enchanting. The day was brilliantly fine but cool, yet with only a scented steaming from the garden to show for the night's rainstorm; the crushed and spent carpet of blossom that lay in great drifts across the darkly green grass. Creamy fragrant frangipani in so many pastel tints, golden trumpets of allamanda, the delicate jacaranda, broken trusses of red poinciana blooms. It looked like a beautiful tangled jungle, the dazzling yellow cascara, the high curtaining banks of pink and white and cerise bougainvillea that flowered so brilliantly lavish and made the North so distinctive. It was beautiful, but after last night Katharine knew it was wild. The wet season brought in the cyclones, violent hurricanes that left a trail of destruction, but for now, the steaming earth and the grass smelled delicious, washed squeaky clean. If only Darin were here!

Determined not to become discouraged, she dressed swiftly, moving softly so as not to wake Sally, very slender and vulnerable in a cool, pretty sundress that lent a tinge of limpid blue to her eyes. There was no one in the hallway, but the sounds of suppressed laughter scurried through the quiet house from the region of the kitchen. Aboriginal laughter, merry and compulsive. She would be able to beg a cup of coffee there—not that she really needed it. She felt the urge to be out of doors, as though the peace of the beautiful morning could shatter at a moment.

Without warning and almost for an answer the study door opened out in front of her and Katharine found herself looking directly into Rada's eyes. Astonishment, anger, a curious look of complicity was at war there. Deep shadows were beneath those eyes, the matt white face perhaps a shade puffy, curiously naked without make-up. Rada's voice was indescribably hostile, fully displaying her feelings.

'Have you taken to spying on me?'

Such anger and injustice weighed heavily on Katharine, but not for her to return that primitive wrath. She spoke quietly. 'Haven't you noticed it's morning? I'm on my way out of doors.'

Rada was in such a nervous state she hardly seemed able to control herself. 'Don't joke with me!'

'I beg your pardon, I'm quite serious.'

'What I do is no concern of yours!' snapped Rada.

'Of course.' Katharine couldn't bear it. She bent her blonde head and hurried past aware of Rada's peculiar fragrance, the full flowing skirt of her loose diamond-patterned smock. She could feel the tension in the older woman, the enmity that lay like an iron bar across Katharine's slender shoulders. Once in the open doorway, Katharine permitted herself to look around cautiously. Rada had already disappeared, and for no clear reason, Katharine began retracing her steps. She had no great knowledge of the layout of the house. It was very large with many rooms radiating out from the central hall, but she did know that particular room was Curt's study. Her eyes were shining in her small, pale face. Such a bitter tang to ruin the spell of the morning.

The door wasn't locked and the room was just as she imagined—sophisticated but workmanlike, comfortable, very much masculine, elegantly personalised; a built-in storage wall, a handsome black leather sofa and wing chairs, a circular sculptured rug in a subdued rust colour over the black slate floor, a collection of gleaming antique firearms housed in a glass-fronted wall fixture, a tiny bar for informal entertaining, an enormous custom-made desk with silver appointments and a huge polished chrome arc light over it, the only strong colour impact in the whole room a magnificent action painting by Sawry, one of his Indian series inspired by a trip to America. It gave Katharine a curious feeling to be in such a room. She switched on the arc light and directed the beam full on the painting, flushing slightly with pleasure. The blue of the sky was the same dense, beautiful blue as her dress, the whole thing forceful and glowing, attracting her most critical attention.

Had Rada too been admiring the painting? Katharine didn't think so. Rada could probably go anywhere she pleased in this big house, but there had to be a reason for this early morning visit. In a way it was quite out of character. Rada was sure to be a late riser and not the sort of woman to be caught dead without make-up. Katharine swung the arc light back again and looked around her, almost searching for something she couldn't see. Rada was a very strange woman, a determined and ruthless woman, and her golden eyes had burned too fiercely bright. There had been a harried air about her as well, a certain eeriness, as though something weighed heavily on her mind. Even her voice would have cut into stone. If it wasn't so absurd, she had seemed both frightened and suspcious of Katharine. The suspicion, at least, was on both sides.

Katharine turned and looked at the desk. The drawers were shut tight, the papers on the desk orderly, not a thing out of place—a confirmation of the man himself. Katharine had no business here, yet she edged a little closer. She could scarcely go through Curt's papers, yet the sight of Rada coming out of the study had strangely upset her, some kind of inbuilt warning. Yet there could be no sinister mystery in this quiet study. What did she expect to find? A report on her brother?

Just inside the doorway, Curt Dangerfield was studying her. His voice was cool, a faintly imperious note in it.

'I didn't expect to find you in my study!'

He looked much bigger and taller this morning, his eyes very green, the cleft in his chin very pronounced.

'Sorry.' Katharine smoothed the feeling of guilt out of her voice. It wasn't the time to go completely to pieces. 'Actually I thought I might find you here.'

'Try again, Katharine.'

'Why else would I be here?'

'You tell me,' he invited.

'You like asking questions!'

He laughed, an attractive sound even if there was no humour in it. 'Damn right I do!'

'But you won't answer them.'

'And you were trying to find some answers here? Shame on you, Katharine!' He moved across the room slowly and sank into the swivel chair, spinning it round to face her. 'There's nothing here that would concern you.'

'I touched nothing.' She stood looking down at him, yet she was clearly on the defensive.

'What would you have liked to have searched for ... *found*?'

She tilted her head away from him, floundering hopelessly. 'I'm too much in the dark.'

She could feel him shake his dark head. 'I've given you the report on Darin.'

'Not all the facts,' she insisted.

'Look at me, Katharine, and sit down.'

'I don't choose to.'

'How odd! You look so sweet and innocent and amenable.'

'Strictly speaking, I am,' she told him.

'I like the sound of that. At least you slept.'

'Yes, I did. I had a visitor—Sally.' She let her eyes encounter his very direct gaze.

'Poor little Sally! What was it, the rain?'

'That, and being left far too much to herself.'

'What would you have me do?' he asked with ironic amusement. 'Come along at one o'clock in the morning?'

Despite herself, she coloured. 'I didn't mean *you*!'

'Do you mean to tell me you don't like me?'

She drew a deep breath. 'I won't say.'

'All right, Katharine, I'll give up my attempt at probing. Let's go out and enjoy the morning.'

She ignored the hint of acid. 'Which is what I started out to do.'

'And what interrupted you?'

'You.'

'I don't believe that. You're just trying to shake me off.'

'Now that would be something. I've got to face this, haven't I? The truth about Darin.'

'Don't condemn him too early,' he said sharply.

'*I* don't. Never me.'

'Who, then?' His voice was dangerously soft.

'Mrs Lewis.'

'Ah!' He let out a long breath, linking his hands

behind his head, tilting back precariously in the chair. 'So we've led up to it. There are no secrets with Rada. Like all women.'

'I wish you'd told me,' said Katharine.

'What was there to tell?' He got up abruptly with the uncanny grace he had, beside her so swiftly she drew a startled breath.

'Don't tower over me. You make me so nervous!'

'I'm quite human!' he said, his eyes narrowing. 'Very human, in fact!' As he spoke he caught the point of her chin and dropped a hard kiss on her mouth.

'Oh!' she said swiftly to cover her confusion, startled at the intensity, the colour and life that slashed through her at just the brief touch of his mouth. Did he think he could do as he liked? Any gesture at any time of his choosing? Colour came into her cheeks and her beauty was very real, though Curt was looking at her now as though he disliked her.

'That's for being in the wrong place at the right time. So look out!'

She moved her head back, barely touching her own quivering mouth. 'You're a pirate! Yes, a pirate. You only need a black patch over one eye.'

The glance that slid over her only discomfited her further, whipping up heat in her veins.

'Why? Because I steal a few kisses? I'm determined to enjoy your company, Katharine, though I can see you're going to give a lot of trouble.'

'Darin is supposed to have stolen cattle.'

'Who told you that? No, *answer* me.'

'You're hurting me!' she complained.

'I'm not. Oh, maybe I am. Your skin is so delicate.'

'Isn't it so?' she asked, rubbing her wrist.

'It could be. I'm not sure, but I'll give you a firm promise. I'll find out. Don't meddle in anything dangerous, Katharine.'

'But you only give me silence.' She lifted her eyes with the sheen of repressed tears in them.

'Don't look at me like that. You're not a hostage. What we all have to wait for is proof.'

'But you did try to spare me the facts?'

'You're not *listening*, Katharine,' he said harshly. 'I said we need proof. Leave the whole thing to me. I promise you whatever Darin's done, we won't send him to prison.'

'What does it really matter to you?'

He twisted her head up but didn't answer immediately. Katharine found she couldn't meet his eyes, so she fixed her attention on a tiny brown button near his lean, darkly tanned throat.

'What marvellous lashes you have, Katharine,' he said with acute mockery.

She swept the same lashes up and gave an involuntary gasp. The man excited her unbearably, and to make it worse he was perfectly aware of it. It was difficult to combat that hard, baffling charm. 'I detest the way you're treating me!'

'Really?'

'Yes, and no way to deny it.'

'Dammit, Katharine, I don't want an argument.

Please just wait. I'm used to obedience.'

'You don't have to convince me of that. All right, Mr Dangerfield, you'll hear no more from me. *Today*'

'Very cordially put. I can see you like scoring off me. I just want to tell you it's a dangerous habit. Let's get out!'

She was trembling slightly. His whole charisma was of such force and vigour that such a reaction might almost be taken for granted. He took her arm, feeling the feathery waves of excitement.

'What the devil——!'

'Oh, leave me alone!' she begged.

'Why, you perverse little witch! You wanted to come here.'

'It's for Darin that I came.'

'And now you're here for yourself!'

She sighed deeply, her silvery-grey eyes enormous. 'I'm rather frightened of you.'

'Yes, and I like it. A healthy reaction. You should be.'

She couldn't say anything, he mesmerized her so much. A man like Curt Dangerfield would always take one's breath away. She spun on her heel, striving for balance. If she wasn't careful, she could inflict a whole lot of punishment on herself. She hadn't expected this, but it had happened, one of life's ironies, her frightening awareness of everything Curt Dangerfield did and said. Some strange magnetism worked between them, a crackle of electricity. His green eyes mirrored it, a certain self-mockery, the sensual twist to his mouth. In many ways he was a damnable man, for she knew in his own way he somehow resented her—a miscalculation when he couldn't think of another.

'Can you ride?' he asked abruptly, as though it would be a forcible shock to him if she said yes. 'Oh, stop looking so heartbreaking!' he taunted her. '*Can* you? Not in that little skimpy dress.' He was propelling her gently into the hallway, instant authority, a golden beam of sunlight hitting his head through the beautiful fanlight. 'Come on, I'll forget our little feud if you will. If you can't ride, we'll go in the jeep.'

'I can ride,' she said, stabbed by his taunting.

'Then go and get changed. Five minutes, no more.'

'I'll wake Sally.'

'Do you want to come?' he asked shortly, seemingly at the end of his patience.

'Oh yes.'

'Well then ... Meet me down at the stables.'.

Half a mile outside the homestead perimeter, a giant fig had been struck in the storm, Beetles swarmed all over it, glittery steel-grey things, with red spots and huge black antennae, laying their eggs on the fresh bark.

'The next generation,' Curt pointed out. 'They beat the opposition with sheer numbers and excreting a poisonous antibiotic.'

'The storm didn't do as much damage as I would have thought,' she commented.

'That was mild.' His glance touched her, jade-green.

'You surprise me.'

'Stay and live through a cyclone or two. They should sweep in from the Coral Sea any time now, but usually January through to March. We've been cut off for weeks with the rivers and creeks swollen and choked with silt and fallen logs. The roads are impassable.'

'Well, it looks very beautiful now,' she observed feelingly. 'The air filled with scent, so many luxuriant blossoming trees. No wonder the lorikeets and the honeyeaters swarm to them.'

'All sweetness is irresistible, Katharine. Most of our rain-forest trees flower now, but don't ride over there. That's the Shining Leaf, the Stinging Tree. The leaves are covered with tiny toxic hairs. You might get a bad sting.'

'That's a good reason.'

'Strangely enough the green possums feed on them, the Nymph butterflies as well. Let's head over towards the lantana. It's a major attraction for our great butterfly colonies. It was brought in as a garden plant from Central and South America. As you can see, it's gone wild.'

'Spectacular walls of it! How dazzling!'

'It's a menace as well,' he said dryly. 'Inpenetrable and as jagged as barbed wire.'

'Do we need to dismount?' Katharine turned to

look at him and her skin tightened electrically. He was the most disturbingly handsome man, all splendid easy arrogance, a superb rider on the most beautiful animal she had ever seen, a coal-black stallion, powerful and fast to ride. Her own horse was a pinto filly called Water Lily with excellent manners, but nothing like the great presence of Jet Master, Curt's horse. Still, his selection was excellent. She would have been over-mounted on the black, if indeed she could have managed him, though she was, as Curt quickly found out, no novice. Learning to ride had been simple with an excellent pony club not far from their home. Once Darin had been its star member, winning all the competitive events. So long ago!

He could see the sudden thought that tormented her. 'Snap out of it, Katharine. You're going to enjoy yourself, remember? We don't need to dismount, as it happens. The butterflies won't mind if we stalk them. The hunting birds don't bother them, either, only the spiders. We all seem to get caught in golden webs.'

Near to the brilliant pink bank of lantana, the butterflies fluttered and darted in an incredible display. Such magic and such an unfamiliar, haunting sight. 'How lovely!' Katharine exclaimed.

There were dozens of Jezebels, white moth-like until they displayed their vivid under-patterns, yellow and black and scarlet; pink and green spotted Triangles and orange and pansy brown Cruisers. The beautiful red Lacewings sailed over the highest bunches of flowers, their deep rose pink into crimson bordered by a velvety blue-black. The largest of them all, the giant Birdwing, a full eight inches across, flopped her brilliant lime and black wings lazily, her yellow body glinting in the sun, but the most spectacular of all to Katharine's dazzled eyes was the beautiful Ulysses, its flashing, beating wings the most intense iridescent blue, bordered by black and scalloped with a delicate tracery of white. It was fascinating watching them touch down lightly on the frail flower clusters, probing flower after flower with long exploring tongues.

It was a moment of enchantment in this wild, lonely place. 'How marvellous! I wouldn't have missed this for the world.'

Curt's eyes narrowed over her rapt profile. She was hatless, a state he didn't want repeated, and her hair fell to one side in a silvery slide. In the bright sunlight her young skin was flawless. 'It's a common sight!'

'It's another world to me.'

'You forgot to say thanks.'

'You make it hard for me,' she explained diffidently.

'Oh! How?'

'By just being you.'

He paused to consider this thoroughly, his eyes flickering across her young face. 'Oh, I see!' He smiled, an extraordinarily attractive smile, very cool and amused.

'I'm doing my best to cover it,' she went on.

'All you can do.'

There was a pulsating silence while he just sat there arrogant as the devil watching her as though she was the most fascinating butterfly of the lot. Discovery was unfamiliar and an agony. Katharine couldn't withstand that green gaze. There was something about him that made her physically breathless. So much easier to concentrate on this brilliant, fluttering spectacle, coloured wings shot through by the sun.

'Had enough?' he enquired lazily. 'Stay here much longer and it might become tiresome.'

Her grey eyes were suddenly pleading. 'Have I annoyed you?'

'I expect in some way you have,' he replied dryly. 'Don't worry, you'll see lots more, but for now, we'll have done and go back for breakfast—not the usual birdseed, by the look of you.'

'I've an average appetite, but please speak freely.'

'I usually do.'

She was aware of the breeze on her face, the pink puff of blossom that rained down on them. 'Race you,' she said, trying to think why she had ever issued such a challenge to this centaur.

'I'll be damned!' His dark laugh reached her and that settled it. Katharine sent Water Lily off at a gallop, greatly exhilarated, racing across the open woodland, her heart hammering, her hair flying. The little pinto was a lovely ride. She would give that arrogant beast a run for his money! She threw a quick look out of the sides of her eyes, increasing her speed, exultant as the filly's lovely long stride lengthened. It was effortless, like the breeze, this going together. What a sweet mover! She was very pleased with herself.

The stallion passed them like a basalt sculpture, going like a jet, its rider lifting one arm high in the air like a supremely confident rodeo rider, so light-hearted, so careless, Water Lily of her own accord just gave up. Whatever it was, it was just no go. Katharine decided to press things no further. All she had to remember was that Curt Dangerfield could beat her at anything.

'Well?' he queried.

'You win!'

'A very wise lady.'

'If you're conceited I suppose you've got cause,' she admitted.

'Thank you.' He bent sideways and bowed. 'As a matter of fact, Katharine, it was the greatest discovery to me that you could ride at all. Which you do very well.'

'You have the superior animal,' she pointed out mildly.

'I've plenty of other horses you can try out. It's a long time since a woman challenged me.'

'Male vanity and pride!'

'Any time.'

'You can be sure I'll get round to it.'

'Said with a very confident air.' The horses had drawn together, the stallion accepting Water Lily's welcoming whinny as his due. Curt ran his fingers over the splendid dark crest. 'When did you begin to ride?'

'When we were children. Darin and I went to the same riding school. We had a very good pony club —that kind of thing. Darin was wonderful!'

The years blurred and ran back and she could see Darin's tawny head thrown back in elation, as he rode over to the judge to salute. Darin flourishing his cap. Too much flamboyance and too little quiet precision. He could never resist it. Top Score, Darin Sutton. He didn't always have control over himself, but he had tremendous control over horses. Oh, Darin! The image of him diminished her pleasure in the day.

'I don't think I can bear it!' she said, her eyes shimmering.

'You're too sensitive,' he said crisply, considering her face. 'You must have been a very lonely child. Some kind of brother fixation when I don't think you learned a great deal about him.'

'I know I'm longing to see him again,' she assured him.

'He never showed much interest in you. Or your mother.'

'There was a time when he was everything to both of us. You can't know.'

'Of course I know! Oh, Katharine, grow up.'

'I might have known you wouldn't be at all sympathetic. It's plain to see you don't need any-one.'

'That's the first time in my life I've heard that.'

His green eyes met hers, very frosty and clear.

'It's all the same anyway,' she shrugged. 'Neither of us can find him.'

'Are you sure you want him found?'

'I'd like to know the truth.'

'All right, take the birds,' he said jarringly. 'That was pretty contemptible!'

'*Now* you give it a name!' Her hair spilled around her flushed face and she tilted her chin.

'You said you wanted to know. Reality is quite different, isn't it, Katharine? No, you're not going anywhere.' He leant over and gathered in the little pinto's reins. 'Darin wasn't the only one, of course. Some even boast about it. I just don't want you to fret about him. Opportunism is his middle name.'

Sheer, primitive, heart-wrenching rage overtook her. She couldn't help herself. Not Darin, the hero figure of her childhood! Her hand flew out involuntarily and Curt grasped it in mid-air, holding it painfully firm. 'Are you so fragile you'll break under the strain? You wanted to talk and I've got no more time to split hairs. *Face* it!'

'You're as good as condemning him!' she insisted.

'For the smuggling, yes. About anything else, I don't know as yet. Easier to let it go, Katharine.'

She was so close to him it was the greatest temptation not to try and hit out at him again. Someone had to be punished for Darin. The sparkling jet of anger was still on her, making her eyes sparkle like gems. She half turned towards him, her hands shaking.

'It's easy to see what's on your mind,' he said sharply. 'Don't try it. *Don't*. I might forget the old maxims.'

'I'll go!' she threatened.

His expression changed elusively. 'I don't know what's got into you. You want to be convinced of Darin's innocence. Stay and be convinced. I'm not sending you away.'

'Why not? You never wanted me here in the first place.'

'True, but I've had a rapid change of heart. All that misguided loyalty is appealing. Maybe I care what happens to that precious white skin. You're too beautiful to throw to the lions.'

'Don't waste your black charm on me,' she said, breathing erratically.

'All right, I'll keep it. No need to panic, Katharine, I'm not going to touch you. Neither will I let anyone else hurt you. Probably I'll wind up with one hell of a headache. It was my intention to let Darin save his own skin.'

'Darin didn't disappear?' She made a strange little sound.

'My darling girl, Darin bolted. Made a run for it.'

'I can't breathe!' she gasped.

'Yes, you can. I'm right here beside you and I think we'll get going. You have the strangest effect on me. Too much excitement before breakfast.'

Her fingers clenched on the reins. 'Do you mind if I make a few inquiries of my own?'

'I realise that was what you were trying to do earlier this morning.'

'That's the trouble—I wasn't!'

'Then I won't have to lock it? My study.'

'Not from me.'

'Ah well, Katharine, keep your mystery. I have to admit it's pretty effective.'

'And it's quite natural. How do you know I didn't follow someone in there?'

'No one goes into my study,' he said with a faint trace of anger, the lines from nose to mouth pronounced, the cleft chin formidable.

'Then I was alone!' Katharine jerked her head back, her wide eyes hurt and distressed. Why didn't she tell him? She had no need to protect Rada, the natural born predator.

Curt bent towards her, his intensely expressive face now coolly sardonic. 'Think no more about it, Katharine. Let's go back. Madonna lilies usually wilt in the sun.'

'Don't concern yourself about me. I won't get sunburnt.'

'Oh, I didn't realise,' he said suavely. 'Your face is quite pink!'

She met that sparkling, mocking glance head on. 'I'm getting to recognise that gleam in your eyes. It's just natural for you to behave outrageously.'

'I like that!' He compressed his curved mouth. 'How have I been saddled with that reputation?

Go on, don't tilt your chin away, tell me?'

'Do you imagine I want a quarrel?'

'Of course you do,' he said leisurely. 'It's been clear from the start. Women are great time-wasters!'

'You suggested this ride!' she said, almost cut to the quick.

'And I'm enjoying it. You've simply no right to look the way you do.'

'And I'm determined to protect myself,' she retorted.

'From *me*?' His green eyes were brilliant between his thick, black lashes. 'Are you saying I'm trying to bewitch you?'

'I'm saying I'm going back to breakfast and sanity.'

'Why chicken out at the last minute?'

'I've too many other things on my mind.' Her face indicated that she had no wish to be drawn further, but he failed to heed its warning.

'Reconsider, Katharine. Half-Moon is really like the Garden of Eden. Why not live here?'

He was smiling with vivid impudence into her face, plainly enjoying her discomfort immensely. 'I'm mature enough to say no to any of your off-beat proposals, Mr Dangerfield.'

He tilted his black head and gave a great shout of laughter. 'Really, Katharine, such a thing never crossed my mind. I'm a very happy bachelor.'

'I'm glad.' She smiled at him, for the first time

with genuine amusement, and he narrowed his eyes at the change in her delicately boned face.

Conversely his own face hardened. 'I think all the bewitching is the other way around.'

The full sunlight on her face suddenly seared like fire. She was shaken by too sharp, unfamiliar desires. He was such an ever-changing tormentor. 'I should have worn a hat,' she managed somewhat plaintively.

'Isn't that what I said in the first place?'

'As it happens, yes. You're a wonder!'

'Thank you, Katharine. That's a beginning!'

She sighed and turned the filly's head towards the caverns of trees. In the distance was a pure stand of fan palms, the giant leaves fully four feet across, beyond that one of the endless chain of lagoons alive with water fowl after the overnight rain-storm. The sound of their squabbling over territorial rights was almost overwhelming. A brilliant blue kingfisher with a fine white tail took off almost in front of them with what appeared to be a small green frog in its scarlet beak.

The exotica of the tropics, Katharine thought, following the bird's flight with her eyes, shading her forehead with the back of her hand. Everything was so lush and prolific—the singular legions of brilliantly coloured birds, the profusely flowering trees, the moon-shaped billabongs, and hovering over them the unique aura of the rain-forest and the distant great dividing line of the indigo ranges. Life was strange, she thought, to bring her up here.

Her heart was racing with over-keyed emotions. So many jumbled thoughts to goad her. She fell into a fraught silence, unaware that the man beside her continued to watch her like a hawk.

CHAPTER FOUR

THE days slid into one another at an alarming rate, all the more alarming because some tightly furled, repressed area of Katharine's life suddenly, shockingly blossomed. A literal change overnight. As Curt had so rightly diagnosed, Katharine had been a lonely, very reticent child, so she was doubly unprepared for her own awakening and the depths and strengths of her nature, intensely feminine, but delicately independent. If Half-Moon somehow kept her a prisoner, it had also freed her. She would have been astounded too to know that even her undoubted beauty had taken on a new dimension as though warm blood now flowed through an ivory statue. The rigid, disciplined routine of her life had been broken.

To be fair, her mother had always loved her, showered on her many advantages, a lovely home, plenty of good clothes, an excellent education and additional refinements, but she had never bestowed the great gift of laughter, sharing one another's thoughts and feelings, the triumphs and setbacks. Had Katharine been eighty instead of eighteen, her mother would still have thought of, and treated her, like a child. Theirs had never been a close relationship, no suggestion of a warm and carefree existence. Life was a burden, the bitterest disappointment. The gods frowned on those they favoured too early.

It had not always been so. It was only after the sudden, needless death of their father (he had been a constructional engineer and killed in a freak accident on a dam site) that their mother had retreated from the world. She had never ceased to mourn her son's defection. Darin was her firstborn, her favourite, he favoured his dead father. Katharine was a mere shadow of her gay, extrovert brother. She had never in her life felt jealousy or envy. In many ways, Darin had been the only real person in their home. Her mother had discouraged young visitors to the home; their voices were too loud, their clothes and manners were appalling, and worst of all they were clumsy. One of Darin's friends had in fact broken a valuable antique through sheer carelessness. After that, it was better not to ask. The house became shrouded in silence.

Katharine's few friends never really cared. Something about her mother's character held them in awe. A handsome, highly intelligent woman, she was only living on the fringe of life, hardly hearing or answering, a neurotic, surrendering long before time. The transition from beloved wife to bereft widow had depleted her limited resources. She was not a fighter, disdained the effort. She had always been more wife than mother. She had rarely left the house save for the occasional concert or ballet or art showing. If any other man in place of her husband even mildly admired her she retreated in shocked outrage. Her husband's death had decided her that the best and important days of her life had departed. Living for so long in such a depressed state, she became ill and died with quite frightening ease.

Katharine, at that time, had been reduced to little more than a silver-haired wraith. Darin had rescued her. They had shared a holiday together and after that he kept her informed of his plans. If he regretted his so-called 'betrayal' (his mother had dubbed it such) he never said so or even touched on the subject. Darin avoided commitments like the plague—such a strange mixture! It had hit Katharine hard to learn that he was less than perfect. More, apart from these fresh accusations, he had taken and kept the gold collar without their mother's knowledge or consent. All small girls tended to romanticise their brothers, and Katharine had been more adoring than most.

Rada had accused him of many things, but oddly Curt seemed loath to publicise the results of his investigations, knowing precisely what Darin meant to his sister. For the tyrant Katharine had once dubbed him, he had shown himself to be surprisingly merciful, though he frowned whenever she mentioned Darin's name. Whatever misdeeds Darin might have been guilty of, his employer seemed prepared to leave in the past, a swift cutting of losses having made certain there would be no more. Katharine considered it likely, though she didn't know why, that it was for her own benefit and continuing peace of mind.

Sally, at least, was profiting from her stay. Unaccountably Rada made no objection to the warm feeling of friendship and liking her small daughter had for their unwanted visitor. For one thing, it allowed Rada to fly out to the Coast for two days. She arrived back with a new hairstyle, golden eyes gleaming, lids flickering with all sorts of silent, satisfactory secrets. For someone who wished Katharine speedily away from Half-Moon, Rada was most selfishly content to wish on Katharine or Martha the care of her daughter—anything, providing Grandma Lewis didn't get the child. Sally, previously left largely to her own devices, now had a friend and confidant. The two girls spent a lot of time together and they were allowed to go wherever they pleased within certain limits of the homestead.

Curt they scarcely saw until dinner. With the approach of the Wet, he was kept very busy with the affairs of the Dangerfield chain. Herds had to be shifted from one property to another and on Half-Moon brought in from the lowland pastures. Flooding creeks and lagoons meant only one thing —drowned stock. So, for an hour each morning, Katharine decided to don her music teacher role, wondering briefly if she could possibly be benefiting Sally if the promise of future lessons was denied her. At least she was doing no harm. If Sally had any real talent it should prove rewarding and a

123

pleasure. The piano was a Bechstein, a concert grand and in excellent condition despite the humid, tropical conditions—no chance thing but the result of constant attention. Like all pianos it was just begging to be played.

Martha, delighted with the whole idea and Sally's champion, swept off the beautiful shawl throwover and opened the instrument up, demonstrating to the two girls' amusement how she careered up and down the keys, pressing down hard here and there, as the piano tuner had shown her, just to give the hammers some necessary work to do. Sally, still giggling and heartened by Martha's inability, played her three-piece repertoire without nervousness. It was enough. Katharine smiled encouragingly on her and took over. It was meant to be the forerunner of a lesson, but somehow it turned into a recital with Martha, Sally on her knee, collapsing into an armchair and loudly professing her wonder.

Sally relaxed, thinking happily that one day she would be able to play like that. Martha, thinking that there was nothing ordinary about Katharine. She was exceptionally well endowed, beautiful and ladylike and charming with best of all a warm, compassionate heart. Poor miserable little Sally had been so much happier since Katharine had arrived, a different child. Katharine was obviously a natural with children and she took excellent care of them. To Martha, at this busy time of the year, about to be run off her feet, it was a wonderful stroke of fate. Of course it was a nagging, ever-present burden, the business about Darin, but there wasn't much point Katharine eating her heart out for a brother who knew only too well how to look after himself.

Martha, understanding her boss, had come to the conclusion that Curt was soft-pedalling the whole thing. Curt was a professional to his finger-tips, the big wheeler-dealer of the cattle world, and he knew a great deal more than he was saying— of that Martha was certain. She had caught him once or twice with a faint look of stress on his face, a hard, implacable flash towards something external, as though he was caught in something he hadn't intended. No doubt their young visitor, so lovely and gentle, was tying his hands. The situation, Martha had to admit, was tricky.

'A miracle!' she said, when Katharine was finished. 'It's just dawned on me, you're a miracle.'

'Oh, well, thank you,' said Katharine, taking the compliment and smiling at Sally, who smiled back. 'Ready for your turn?' she asked.

'Yes, please!' Sally jumped up off Martha's knee and went to the piano, settling herself beside Katharine on the long rosewood seat. 'You make it sound so easy.'

'It isn't terribly hard if you love it.'

'Oh, I do! Honestly, I suffered when I left Miss Murray, and she didn't play half so well as you.'

'That's very generous of you, Sally,' smiled Katharine.

'It's true.'

'At this point I'll leave you,' Martha announced.

'If you're still going on that picnic I'll have that lunch box ready for you.'

'Thanks, Martha.' Katharine looked over her shoulder and smiled. 'Sally knows where we can find some greenhood orchids. We might take a dip in the stream.'

'Well, don't go near the waterfall. Look at it from the other side.'

'Will do. Now, Sally, there's one thing we must get right from the very beginning, the position of the hands.'

From the one or two thunderstorms, all the creeks had begun swelling and Katharine got some idea of what to expect from the monsoon and its companion, the tropical cyclone. But now as she looked around her, she was held captive in a mesh of enchantment. The stream they had chosen was exceedingly beautiful, overhung by trees packed with birds. A greeny-gold light filtered through the branches, spilling gently on the tiny greenhood orchids that sprang up at the base of the knotted trunks. The sandy banks and the stream were strewn with boulders with moss on the rocks, the mirror-clear water exhilaratingly cold as the girls plunged into it, sucking in their breaths. Much further downstream was the waterfall and the deepest pool of all, but Katharine needed no word of caution not to take Sally near it. There the water boiled and bubbled and leapt in a fast-flowing rush over the series of boulders that acted as rapids. It might look the perfect backdrop for some exotic shot of the tropics, the silvery glittering cascades of water, the white foam and the deep emerald pool beneath, but Katharine knew danger lurked there.

Downstream she cut through the water with clean, neat strokes, then she turned over and floated on her back, ash-gold hair trailing, half closing her eyes in sheer physical abandon. Such an idyllic, secluded haven! Sally, too, was splashing in ecstasy, flowers tucked behind her ears, every chicken bone showing, making a small green frog leap up a tree in alarm. Surprisingly, instead of croaking, it gave out a clear bell tone, which Katharine later found out was quite common. It was like being lighter than air and the sky was the most heavenly colour Katharine had ever seen.

'It's like a dream, isn't it?' Sally asked, smiling brilliantly, flicking and puffing at a butterfly. Katharine had never heard her laugh so much.

She pulled herself out of the water and began sunning herself on a rock, her long hair trailing down her back like a mermaid, already drying, and the splashes of sunlight gilding her graceful limbs. She tilted her head back and arched her throat to the sun.

'I want to remain here all my life,' she said blissfully.

'You're serious, I hope!'

The voice was masculine, spiked with mockery, unmistakable. She struggled briefly with shock, then gave up. Curt was coming very fast down the bank, incredibly nimble for a big man, green eyes sliding over her lovely exposed skin. It seemed to Katharine that he was looking at her as no man had ever looked at her before.

'The plot thickens!' Sally surprisingly crowed and waved a glistening hand. 'Hello there, Uncle Curt.'

'Greetings, young Sally. Forgive me for interrupting you, Katharine,' the cattle baron bowed, 'but I just had to follow all the laughter. It floats quite a way!'

Katharine tried to return his lazy admiring glance, but only succeeded in blushing, seemingly turned to quicksilver, her blood molten.

'You're very welcome on your own land,' she said, looking harried.

'I like your swimsuit, Katharine,' he pointed out with maddening precision, his green eyes more green than ever. 'It's very becoming—what there is of it.'

'For your interest, I have two or three more.'

'Heavens!' he shrugged his powerful shoulders. 'I like that one well enough.'

Pantherlike, he moved to her side preparing to share the same wide, sunny rock, his attention momentarily diverted

'I say, Sally, what *are* you doing?'

'Admiring a frog. It's all right, Uncle Curt, he's the dearest little thing in the world. Speckles all over his thighs!'

'That's not your story, Katharine, not a mark on

you. The speckles are for camouflage,' he stressed for Sally's benefit.

'Don't worry, I won't wake it. It's just dozing on this leaf. Just have a look at the eyelids.'

'If you don't mind, I'll stay right here with Katharine. She's frightened of frogs.'

'That's all right!' Sally retorted obligingly. 'I'm not coming out anyway. This is super.'

Curt turned back to Katharine, who was inching out of reach. 'You look worried, Katharine. Didn't you want me to join your swimming party?'

Her eyes slid rather shyly over his profile. Classic, really—a fine brow, straight nose, a good mouth and chin. Strong and distinctive. 'Don't be silly,' she said dizzily. 'I'm very pleased to see you. You can share our lunch if you like.'

'Marvellous! I'll avail myself of that offer. It's not every day I can expect it.'

'Could you pass me my jacket?'

'Why?' he asked softly. 'When a girl looks like you, she shouldn't be at any pains to hide it.'

'Please, Curt,' she said, and the breeze whipped silky strands of her pale hair across his hand.

'I'd much prefer you didn't, but if you'd rather!'

He reached back and collected the light yellow kimono jacket, holding it for her as she thrust her arms into it, tying the sash tightly, like armour.

'You win again,' he said lightly.

'What does that mean?'

'Even with bare feet I like you. Now, where's the food? I'm hungry.'

'I suppose you really need more,' she said thoughtfully.

His hand shot round her wrist and held it. 'Say that again ... !'

'I suppose we won't have enough,' she explained patiently, her grey eyes as clear and innocent as dawn. 'To feed you, I mean.'

For a maddening moment he looked down at her, then he allowed her to pass him, making for the blanket she had planted at the foot of a bush willow. He watched her in silence, then subsided into the shade, all six feet two of him, green eyes a shocking colour in the bronze sheen of his face, lighting a cigarette and drawing on it deeply. After a minute he dropped down to the grassy bank, lying full length, cradling his midnight black head under one hand. His cream, wide-brimmed slouch hat had already taken a wonderfully accurate ride to a convenient peg in the cabbage tree. He looked completely at one with his environment, vivid and somewhat unpredictable.

Katharine deftly spread out the rug and flung a crisp checkered linen square over it, then set out the contents of the cooler: roast chicken, curls of pink ham, crisp salad in a plastic box, the dressing kept separate until the last minute, freshly baked rolls that were golden on the outside and white and tender within, a home-made lemonade for Sally, and a Thermos of coffee for Katharine accompanied by spicy chunks of Martha's best ginger cake.

'Are you ready to join us?' invited Katharine.

'Right!' Curt said briefly, and opened his eyes.
'Sally?'

'Do I have to come yet?' Sally complained.

'Not if you don't want to. I'll keep a plate for you.'

'Just a drumstick, that's all I want!' Sally told them. 'Oh, and my lemonade and a piece of Martha's cake.'

'That's all?' Curt called across to the child. 'I'm ready to start when you are, Katharine.' His green eyes were taunting, aware of the colour under her skin that wasn't put there by the sun.

She almost felt dizzy, as she passed him the highest piled plate, neatly tucking her long legs to the side opposite him.

'What are you trying to do, hide?' he queried.

'Haven't you somewhere else to look?' she retaliated.

'All right, Katy, I'll take no further notice of you. Where's the salt?'

'Didn't I salt it?'

'No.'

'I thought I did.'

'Obviously, but you're not yourself.'

'And you know me so well?' she asked.

'So well it hurts.'

She accepted this in silence, then sidetracked. 'Would you care for some mustard?'

'Trying to make conversation?'

'Yes. You do it on purpose, I know that. Trying to torment me.'

'Come on, Katy,' he drawled, 'that's an outrageous statement!'

'I thought you didn't like abbreviations?'

'Katy will do for a start.'

'If only you would explain yourself.' She gave a little shiver, turning fully to face him.

'Curiosity killed the cat, Katy. I know. Now eat up. No girl should completely forget that a man likes a few curves.'

'Are you saying I'm not ample enough?' she demanded.

'Keep your pride. I'd offer you a contract if I were looking for star material.'

'It's no use!' she said finally. 'You must have been a terrible little boy, teasing and taunting!'

'It keeps one alive sometimes. Besides, there were never sweet little girls around in my day. Only Grandma.'

'There've been plenty since.'

'*Mea culpa!* I wish I could deny it, but you have to remember, a thirty-five-year-old bachelor! As a matter of fact, a very dear friend of mine is flying in for the week-end—Jo-Ann Macauley. She's good fun. Plenty of glamour, but lively. You'll like her. We'll make up a party and spend a night in the rain-forest. It should prove quite educational. If you don't see it soon it will be too late for this year. Once the rain starts, that's it!'

'Curt?' Her voice was low, pleading, obviously trying to humour him.

He lifted his head, alert, and for a moment his

expression had a black brooding. Even his eyes darkened. 'When you start off like that, I can guess what you want to say. Don't bother me today with Darin. This is a pretty good lunch, so let's get on with it. It's been a twenty-four-hour day of late.'

'I'm sorry. You do work hard.'

A crooked smile played about his curvy mouth. 'Thank you. How could I fail to accept such a charming apology? Pour me some coffee like a good girl.'

'Yes, master.'

'That's the way of it, Katy.'

'Well, well, well!' she smiled.

'At least I'm not leading you on in ignorance.'

'Three teaspoons of sugar, right?'

'You remember.'

'It's very dangerous, all that sugar.'

'You can say that again! May I have a slice of that ginger cake? Martha is very lavish with her helpings, but you're something else again!'

She passed it to him very absentmindedly and he tugged at her hair. 'What's wrong?'

'I'm fine. Fine.'

'You were when I arrived,' he said shortly.

'It's not *you*,' she answered low-voiced.

He gave a deep sigh, not the man for suffering fools gladly or encouraging weaknesses. 'That's the worst of families,' he said, staring up at the sky-light through the trees. 'They're almost inter-changeable. Let Darin back out of his own tight corners. Why have you got to get in there with him? Don't worry it to death. No good will come of it. *Please.*'

She swung fully towards him, almost involuntarily, into his arms. There was scarcely a breath of space between them. 'What then am I doing here?'

'Enjoying yourself!' he answered almost with violence, not touching her but looking at her so intently she felt dizzy. 'I would say there's been precious little enjoyment in your young life.'

'Why do you say that?' She had to look away from him, bending her head forward, curtaining her face.

'If I hadn't been a cattle man I might have been a doctor. You see, Katy, you interest me.' Curt put out a lazy finger and hooked the silky swing of her hair behind her ear. 'There, that's better! Do you want to talk to me about your mother?'

'As a matter of fact, no.'

'Poor Kat! You will. Bottling things up can be hell. It's my view that you're very repressed. Improving, but still a long way to go.'

'You know how I feel about Darin,' she said quietly.

'I'm on *your* side, not Darin's,' he said with a flash of sharply etched anger.

'Why mine?'

'There's so much less of you,' he drawled, back to a smile again. 'And what's there, I like!'

'You're dreadful!'

'That sounds familiar. I think you mean, Katy, I'm different from what you're used to and I won't let you wallow in this adolescent passion for your brother.'

'You're a very hard, dynamic man,' she said gravely, reflectively, almost speaking to herself.

'In a minute we'll be in each other's arms.'

'Actually I'm only speaking in honesty. No come-on intended.'

'I know that!' he flicked her a green, lancing glance. 'Answer me, fair Katharine, have there been any suitors for your hand? Any unspeakable affairs?'

'I'm not as exciting as you are.'

'Nonsense!' He put down her coffee mug carelessly and a shiny blue beetle immediately flew into it. 'That's not true!'

'There was one person I was very fond of!' she admitted.

'That sounds delightful. *Fond?*'

'He was hardly more than a boy,' she protested, annoyed by his suave, sardonic tone.

'What difference does that make?' he pointed out reasonably. 'You may think of me differently, but I was once a boy myself.'

'He was nothing like you,' she said feelingly, and even shuddered, a sweet little ripple down her spine.

'I'm grateful for that!' he said dryly. 'You look what you are, Katharine—extremely tender and sheltered. I'm very taken with you when I didn't think I would be.'

'I detested the sound of you,' she responded, thinking it was perfectly true.

'And now look at us! Such a surprise!'

'Are you ever serious?' she asked.

Curt allowed himself to lean back on the bank and look up at her, his sparkling eyes intensely alive. Her silver-gilt hair streamed round her shoulders. Shining hair. Shining eyes. Shining skin. Graceful as a swan and in some ways just as innocently remote. 'Am I ever serious?' he repeated softly. 'Honest to God, yes!'

'You'd never think so!'

One minute she was sitting upright, watching him, the next, pinned down on the thick carpet of grass. 'What good would it do me, Katy?'

She was swallowing convulsively, her cloud-grey eyes showing an exquisite kind of panic.

'You see,' he said lightly, 'one has to encourage little birds to eat out of the hand. You've got a lot to learn.'

'Sally's watching.' It sounded like an appeal.

'No, she's not. I've excellent vision, even in the back of my head. Why are you so frightened of me?' he asked, his eyes falling to her thudding heart.

'I'm glad you realise.' There was real shock in her eyes and she had never looked more beautiful.

'A foolish question really!' He moved quickly, his hand in the small of her back, lifting her up again. 'We both know why.'

'Nothing to do with Darin, as it happens,' she whispered, completely off-balance, aching.

'I'm quite aware of that. There's a simple, effective way of handling you, Katharine, but for obvious reasons I must proceed with caution.'

'The happy bachelor?' Her head was whirling and the words almost hurt her.

'Now why is a bachelor regarded with suspicion? Pretty nearly every woman I meet wants to change that.'

'*I* don't!' she said with shocked emphasis.

'Be that as it may, Katharine ...' He suddenly stood up, towering over her, the sunlight like a bar of gold across his brown throat. There was an odd silence for a minute while he continued to look down at her, then he moved abruptly and extended his hand. 'Rise, girl, this is all very distracting, but I've more important things to do.'

'I'm not a child to be entertained!' she said crossly.

'Yes, you are.'

She swayed a little and he put a steadying hand on her shoulder. 'One day I may change it.'

'No!' she protested automatically, and his hand encircled her white nape.

'Good. We understand each other!'

'I'll never understand you.' Her sensitive face was shadowed, softly, innocently ravishing.

'That's what you tell *me*,' he said curtly. 'But you're not convincing yourself. Don't try to detain with all this delicate beguilement, I'm very busy with my work!'

'I wonder you took such a short time off!' she said over-emotionally.

'Don't cry.'

'I'm not. How ridiculous!' He was so much under her skin she was surrendering by the minute.

'Your eyes are shimmering,' he pointed out. 'Really, Katharine, they're the ultimate in seduction, whether you know it or not.' He tapped her cheek with a stinging finger that actually left a mark. 'But like I said ... more urgent matters call.'

He began to walk up the bank, idly collecting his wide-brimmed hat. She betrayed her own resolution not to call after him.

'Do you mean that about taking me to the rain-forest?'

'You bet!' he drawled laconically, intensely male, hard and alert, green eyes flicking back to look over her. 'Understand, Katy, I'll have to ask a few other people along. Alone with you I might forget all my training!'

'It's a lot to ask you to stop all this nonsense!'

'Silly child! In reality I'm behaving very suitably. I don't talk like this with everyone.'

'You've broken dozens of hearts!' she accused him.

'Granted!' He gave a white grin. 'So long, sunflower. Sally!' he called to the madly splashing child, 'I have to go now.'

'See you, Uncle Curt. I've got the prettiest little frog to show you, but never mind.'

'Katharine will come and admire it. Goodbye,

Katy, you look entrancing staring up at me like that. I like you in yellow!'

'Well, green eyes are absolutely devilish!'

'That's my girl!' He laughed outright and briefly saluted her, then continued his course up the bank, whistling up the black stallion that instantly came to him.

Katharine could, if she were quite silly, fall madly in love with him, with no restraint. He was that kind of man, with all sorts of things going for him. A high degree of perfection, a rare technique with a woman. It was a good thing she was so reserved. Even the lightest emotional entanglement with a man like Curt Dangerfield could leave her scarred, in every way different. She put her hands to her cheeks, felt their warm flush, and immediately a hundred little fears struck her. To speak about barriers was one thing, but how did one achieve them?

Standing alone in the centre of the silver stream, unaware of Katharine's frightened speculations Sally was calling:

'Oh, do come! You can't imagine all these brilliant little speckles!'

Katharine walked back to the water's edge, moving gracefully like a ballet dancer or the crane called a brolga. The monsoon was coming and a lot was to happen to her then.

CHAPTER FIVE

Jo-Ann Macauley was a natural anywhere. A tall,
sparkling brunette, not overly glamorous, but just
right, very pleasant and friendly, huge pansy brown
eyes and unabashedly marriage-minded—her long-
time friend, Curt, to be exact. Far from backing
away from her determined and dedicated pursuit,
he appeared to enjoy her company immensely.
They were both witty and worldly with beautifully
polished manners, both members of the landed
gentry with much the same background. As well,
Jo-Ann was really a delightful person. No one could
help liking her. The whole house was caught up in
her irrepressible gaiety.

She arrived with far too much luggage, inspiring
one of Rada's habitual waspish comments, but went
on to shower everyone with presents, including
Katharine whom she had never expected to meet;
hurling 'trousseau gear, darling!' at Curt, Italian
silk shirts, neckties and even a gold medallion pen-
dant which he had promptly hurled back as out of
character, though he accepted the rest and
thoroughly kissed her. Sally sat dazed and pink with
pleasure amid six or seven dolls in national cos-
tume, and even Rada approved her precious bottle
of perfume. Jo-Ann was anything but stingy. She

was a striking-looking, generous-hearted woman, taking her thirtieth year beautifully in her stride.

Katharine knotted her beautiful swirl of a French scarf round her throat and smiled, thanking Jo-Ann prettily, after an initial disclaimer which Jo-Ann refused to acknowledge. Despite Rada's tedious manner, very wearing to the outgoing, Jo-Ann was never happier than to be on Half-Moon. Six months in Europe was wonderful, to be sure, but she was glad to be home. Rada managed to inquire sweetly if there wasn't someone else who needed her, but Jo-Ann, well aware of Rada's peculiar disposition, let such comments slide off her back like bath oil. Jo-Ann was committed to liking most people, and those she couldn't she charmingly ignored.

Not surprisingly Katharine found herself laughing continuously over dinner—funny little anecdotes that occurred to Jo-Ann by the minute or were prompted by Curt, the results of her recent travels and various misadventures. Always the unforeseen element that came along to upset the routine. Katharine found herself relaxing, content to listen to the winged exchanges between Curt and his much admired house-guest. Rada, from her face, didn't appear to be deriving the same pleasure. Rada liked to be the centre of attention and it seemed likely that she might have to wait for hours, days even. Jo-Ann hadn't said how long she would be staying, and the only one who saw fit to ask her, Rada, had somehow not received an answer.

Jo-Ann gave the impression that she had never even heard the question, but Katharine remarked the slight, significant tightening of her full, luscious mouth. Rada, in whatever background, would make things unnecessarily complicated. It seemed to be her life's motivation, and Jo-Ann without ever inquiring had come by the fact that Rada was broke—broke by the Lewis or Dangerfield and even her own standards. She and Jeff must certainly have lived it up for what pitifully short time Jeff had had. Jo-Ann had known him well. In the early days before Rada she had even gone out with him. Jeff had been very attractive, but he couldn't hold a candle to his cousin, as the saying went. Jo-Ann had an extensive list of male friends, but not a one of them seemed interesting beside Curt. He was the sort of man who made a woman know what she was designed for—extraordinary. Every time she saw him, it hit her like a wave.

'Gosh, there's not much left!' she exclaimed, tilting the near empty wine decanter.

'I can get more if you're desperate,' Curt said indulgently.

'Don't worry, darling. A liqueur with my coffee, out on the veranda with the blossoming stars. They don't have stars like that in Europe. Are we all coming?'

'I'll see to the coffee, then I have work to do,' Martha rejoined lightly. Silence from Rada, her golden eyes flashing specks of a moody spirit. Katharine smilingly declined, saying she had promised to look in on Sally. It was a pleasure just to look at their visitor. Not everyone would wear scarlet and still triumph, but on Jo-Ann it sang, just a slither of jersey with an adventurous plunge, lending a glow to her bright, observant eyes, a sheen to her olive, blusher-lit skin.

'Later, then, dear,' Jo-Ann said kindly. 'The night has only begun. What do you say, old buddy, shall we go out on the veranda and hold hands?'

'What's wrong with here?' Curt asked mildly.

'It's not the same!' Jo-Ann groaned. 'I've waited half my life for you.'

'More or less. A few interludes between.'

'Who are they?' she cried. 'My God, all joking aside, who are they? Honestly, honey, you're my ideal. I searched the continent for just such a man.'

'I should have thought so,' he said dryly.

'Well, that's the general idea, darling. What would you have me do? Pine?'

'Never mention the word. I doubt if you'd know how.'

'Damn it all, Curt, does it make that much difference? Tell me, darling, I'm here now.'

'Well, flutter up and be charming.' He held her chair and she immediately jumped up and embraced him.

Katharine stood like a silver birch, Rada like a prophet of doom, possessed by a seething cauldron of resentments.

'Coming, Rada?' Jo-Ann waved her shapely arms in all directions.

'Love to,' Rada responded tightly, knowing there was no better weapon than her presence.

Jo-Ann did not collapse. A visitor she might be and Rada almost on her home ground, but Jo-Ann remained calm. It was a Macauley asset. There had been plenty of times since she had arrived when she had felt like pushing Rada off the roof, but not the slightest sign of it lurked in her eyes or her warm, drawly voice. Katharine, who had very gracefully and tactfully disappeared, she had liked on sight. Dressed properly, the girl would be absolutely ravishing—not that she didn't look bewitching in a simple turquoise long skirt and a pin-tucked cream georgette blouse. Such a beautifully balanced body could carry such a willowy outfit.

Rada preferred things with more zing to them. Rada, as usual, was turned out beautifully. That she loathed the girl, Katharine, Jo-Ann had instantly perceived—not that Rada didn't actively dislike most of her own sex. Still, Jo-Ann turned back to smile at Curt's least likeable relative as though she was dying to discuss every last thing with her. The perfect woman friend, clamping down hard on her very natural frustration at not having Curt to herself. *Yet*! She had never been able to overdo it with Curt. In fact, she had the strongest suspicion that he only needed women for colour. If she played her cards right, she just could be the mother of his children, but she would have to hurry up about it. Childbirth was never easy, and she was not as young as she once had been.—It was all she had ever really wanted out of life—Curt and his children, a lovely homestead, a vast property, plenty of animals about, horses and dogs and cattle. No problem. Rada, however, had been on Half-Moon too long. It wasn't, Jo-Ann considered, that she was just rotten lazy and a fearfully callous mother, Rada was trying to make something of herself. She wasn't born into all this, Jeff had slipped in his standards in more ways than one, and Rada was out for Curt's patrician blood. She was herself—not that he had consented to marry anyone, but Jo-Ann felt she had a better chance than most. It was her own and her mother's honest opinion, and she didn't allow too many virtues to interfere with her pleasure or plans. If Rada wanted a fight, Jo-Ann wasn't ashamed to give her one. Rada was already acting as mistress of the household, and funny as it was, it couldn't be allowed to continue.

Sally was very pleased that Katharine had come to look in on her. Katharine was no longer a visitor but a dear friend. She sat up in bed in a clean blue nightdress, watching Katharine move gracefully around the room collecting some scattered Lego pieces and putting them back in their box.

'It seems a shame you didn't finish this. It was very good.'

'I didn't have enough wheels for the bus,' Sally explained.

'Still, it was good.'

'What do you think of Jo-Ann?' Sally asked, propping herself up on one elbow.

Katharine looked across at her and smiled briefly. 'I like her. She's very nice and friendly.'

'Mother couldn't *possibly*!' said Sally.

'Why not?'

Sally made a lunge for the end of the bed. 'Guess.'

'No,' Katharine said resolutely.

'All right, I'll tell you. Jo-Ann's in love with Uncle Curt.'

'Well? That's pretty obvious, Sally.'

'So's Mum.'

'They can't *both* be,' said Katharine reasonably.

'That's what I say. What's going to happen now?'

'Let's not interfere with anyone's plans,' Katharine said lightly. Not for the world would she have told Sally that she thought Curt Dangerfield regarded women as pawns.

'Jo-Ann is very determined...'

'Listen, darling...' Katharine broke in.

'Please let's discuss it, Katy—I'm worried.'

'I don't think your Uncle Curt wants to get married at all.'

'Oh, I hope so! He's really marvellous. At least he'll always let me come here. He told me. The first time I ever saw him he said: "Hi, chicken!"'

'It's his way to dazzle the female,' explained Katharine.

'Don't you like him?' Sally asked in surprise.

'Of course I do.' I could very nearly love him, Katharine thought to herself. Another one. She

146

turned her head away because her own face was reflected in the mirror. It looked very soft and revealing. Sally evidently thought so too, because her expression became owlish.

'You'd make Uncle Curt a beautiful bride,' she said.

'Why, bless your little heart, I'd be the last woman in the world your dear uncle would light on.'

'Why do you say that?'

'This is a silly conversation, Sally.' Katharine leaned forward and kissed the child. In some respects Sally was too bright. 'First of all, he certainly hasn't told me he loves me.' She began to laugh and Sally joined in. 'And I will *never* love him.'

'I think you're very fond of him,' Sally said, determined to pursue the point.

'What a child! You may have noticed, my pet, your uncle Curt treats us both pretty much the same.'

'He doesn't *look* at us the same.'

'That's irrelevant.'

'I don't think so, and neither does Mother. In any case, *I* love you.'

'You're the dearest, sweetest little girl and I can certainly agree that your uncle Curt will always look after you. You're very lucky!'

'There! What did I tell you?' Sally cried triumphantly.

'You *are* in a funny mood.'

'I'm in a good mood,' Sally said sincerely.

'Then sleep well. Another piano lesson in the morning. You're coming on nicely.'

'I'll never be as splendid as you,' Sally sighed.

'Oh, I don't know. Just keep at it.'

'If Mummy lets me.'

'I'm sure she will, dear, you're so good.'

'Would you speak to her?'

'She's made no objections so far,' Katharine told the child, not wishing to commit herself to a conversation with Rada.

'I am good, aren't I?' Sally said with dignity. 'Maybe if I'm very good at something Mummy will be proud of me.'

'She's proud of you now.'

'No, she's not,' Sally retorted with great conviction. 'She thinks I'm pretty ugly.'

'Oh, don't say that, Sally.' Katharine turned back in distress. 'No child in this world is ugly, and you've been blessed with many assets. You're sweet and you're clever and when you grow up you're going to turn heads. Any woman can learn to look attractive. A pretty face is far from everything.'

'Yes, but it takes such a long time for anyone to look further.'

'You *have* noticed that your uncle Curt is excessively fond of you. Martha is. I am. Believe me, your mother cares for you. Some people just aren't that capable of showing emotion.'

'Boy, you've never seen her angry!'

'Don't hurt yourself, Sally. *Gently*, darling, gently

all your life. You combine a lot of things. You don't have to be obvious.'

'Blue eyes and blonde curls?' Sally asked, putting her thumb in her mouth and rolling her eyes.

'Exactly. Now it's time for your magic sleep. You're on a bed of goose feathers. Goodnight, pet, see you in the morning.'

' 'Night, Katy.' Sally struggled briefly, then fluttered back on to the piled-up pillows. She was very thin and her hair was a mess, but if she wanted to she could be a swan—Katy had made that quite clear. Underneath her wispy brown hair was a good brain. It shouldn't be too difficult. Everyone said she favoured Grandma, and if she turned out like Grandma she wanted nothing more. Tears stung her eyes for a moment. It was always so when she thought of Grandma Lewis, but if she was a good girl and patient, Uncle Curt promised she would get to see Grandma before long. Things weren't easy for Uncle Curt. Oh yes, she knew about Mother's plans even if Katy didn't. Katy wouldn't be serious, but Sally saw in her the very lady Uncle Curt might wish to marry. Mother would be furious. She went up like burned paper and that was the only part Sally didn't like. She moved on the mattress, resting her cheek on her hand, and started with fervour to think of beautiful things. Katy had taught her that—and what's more it worked!

In the Blue Drawing Room, so called because so much blue had been used as a mood-setter,

Katharine turned back the lid of the Bechstein and sat down on the long brocade-covered seat. Small bronze winged figures stood on either side of the music stand holding aloft a bright flare of light. Beyond the piano stood a fine lacquered screen, so tall it was almost ceiling-high, flowers and trees and birds and Oriental figures. An elegant blue rug covered the centre of the polished floor, there were several beautiful formal chairs all covered with a distinctive blue and white silk and a much more re-laxed, deeply comfortable custom-built sofa piled up with silk cushions, side tables, a pair of Chinese Chippendale gilded mirrors, a collection of small canvases, part of the continuing collection found through the house.

Coming back through the central hallway she had heard the sound of voices from the veranda—Jo-Ann's husky laugh, Rada's faintly caustic tones, the dark murmur of Curt's, the tinkling of ice in a tumbler. She would be disturbing nobody here and it was much too early for bed. She would like to do as Sally asked and speak up on her behalf, but she knew only too well any opinion of hers would only antagonise Rada. If anyone was to speak to Rada it would have to be Curt. Busy so much of the time, he wouldn't know just how much progress Sally was making. The child was a natural with considerable manual dexterity and an affinity with the keyboard. It didn't happen that often, and when it did, such potential had to be recognised. Sally badly needed self-confidence and to really shine at something, the piano, for instance, would be excellent therapy. Any suggestions, however, would have to come from Curt. He was the one who would have to play the positive role.

As an experiment, the lessons were already enriching Sally's young life and all the dull little patches she had suffered were being channelled into an engrossing artistic pursuit. Sally, in short, was a born pianist and had Katharine known her background better she would have discovered that this was not so unusual. The Lewis family, the womenfolk in particular, were all music-lovers and each had been given the opportunity to develop above average talent. Sally had in fact told Katherine that it had been 'Grandma' who had arranged for her to have lessons in the first place. Her mother had been perfectly indifferent and was in actuality tone-deaf. Poor little Sally, she was certainly handicapped with a mother like Rada.

Katharine's hand tenderly embraced the bronze nymph, then dropped to the keyboard. Eyes closed, her mood changing, she began to pick out a melody, then fill in the chords with her left hand, very skilfully. It had always been a trick of hers, improvisation. Just the merest outline of something, but it was clearly, essentially, romantic. She should be ashamed of herself. Night-time was always the worst time for this kind of feeling. She should be out on the veranda drinking Tia Maria or whatever it was Jo-Ann had ordered up with her coffee. Not that she had any desire to join the group. Either woman,

Jo-Ann or Rada, would be extremely lucky to find herself for a moment alone with Curt. Sally was right—both of them had their minds a good deal on the same subject. It would be a hard fight. Katherine smiled just to think of it.

The lovely, faintly melancholy little melody grew under her hands, slender, long-fingered, but certainly not frail. Her wrists were strong from long years of practice. A pool of golden light fell all about her, enhancing her downbent blonde head. Absorbed, she was merging with the atmosphere. Half-Moon. The tropical wind, the scented Queen of the Night, the flowering stars, unbelievably big, the luxuriant great ferns of the rain-forest, the swift-running gullies, the floating blue lilies on the lotus ponds ... It was tranquillised yet haunting music, with here and there a gleaming thread of excitement. Something was burning inside her. A soft flame. It was spreading to her fingers, exposing her heart. It was hopeless! Soon it would be all over. She would go away again, for in truth the harm was already done.

'Don't stop!' It was an order, given with alarming gentleness.

She remained as she was, motionless, the light on her hair, a shiver starting at her nape. 'You startled me!' she exclaimed.

'I'm ready to apologise if you'll turn round and look at me.'

He was sitting behind her on the deep sofa, utterly

relaxed, his iridescent eyes with such a claim on her she couldn't turn away again.

'How silently you move,' she said. 'Like a tiger in a jungle.'

'And that's exactly how you're looking at me. I assure you I'm not nearly so dangerous. Since when did you play the piano so beautifully?'

'That's a very pretty compliment indeed.'

'No compliment, Katy, the truth.'

'Why aren't you outside with the others?' Her soft voice was faintly shaded with mockery.

He responded with a spiked glance. 'My darling child, I always feel saddened by feminine malice. Not yours, of course, you're as good as you're beautiful—*naturally*. Rada. She's busy insulting a few people in high places, most of them Jo-Ann's bosom friends.'

'Oh.'

'Yes, oh.' Curt shrugged his wide shoulders, his green glance travelling over her. 'We'll escape in a minute. Pick that melody up again. What is it?'

'Three guesses.'

'Not something of your own. Katy, I'm filled with awe.'

'I know you too well.'

'You don't, but let it pass.'

Her head tilted to one side as she considered. 'I don't really know if I *could* start all over again. Sometimes it comes and just as quickly goes. I lose my powers.'

'Well, that proves it, if it needed proving at all. You're a witch!'

His black hair curled crisply to his head, his eyes as green as a deep pool, lamp-glossed bronze skin accentuated by his pale shirt—one of the Italian shirts Jo-Ann had bought him. He was too attractive to be respectable and she felt like telling him so. 'Have no fears, Katy, I'm not going to kiss you.'

'Such a sense of humour!'

'Don't you want me to?'

'No.'

'I'd like you to remember that. You are, without question, a poor liar.'

Barely seeming to move, he had his arm out holding her while she sat staring up at him seemingly in thrall. 'It seems to me, Katy, you were playing a love song. Perhaps you feel it around you.'

'Enjoy your teasing while you can, because I'm going!'

'*Are* you? You're coming with me. I can always apologise later.'

It was almost a compulsion, a feeling that she didn't really know about to resist him. 'That's impossible!'

'Don't tell me you'd rather be by yourself. That's anti-social. Come with me, Katy, I'm lonely.'

'*Lonely*? You?'

'It's the way I feel.' He tightened his grip on her.

'I can't believe it. In what way do you mean?'

'Oh, this! ... I need you specifically, Katherine.' His hand slid under her chin and he turned her mouth up and kissed it, taking everything, victory, initiative, so extraordinarily bitter-sweet it was impossible to get close enough to him, nothing violent, but urgent, so that she turned fully into his arms, allowing him an inevitable surrender. If it was an impulsive or calculated gesture, it was now neither, but enormously exciting, and she knew she was sliding out of control. Simple, much simpler to allow him to press her still closer to his lean, hard body. The myriad sensations were too much for her—such an infinite variety, his mouth and his caressing hands.

She was breathing deeply, her creamy skin flushed, eyes closed, lost in this swift tide of feeling. There was no gulf between them, no problems.

Curt pulled his head away, standing there just holding her.

'Isn't this what you wanted?' she whispered.

'It happened. It's not enough, Katharine.'

She couldn't say anything. She shook her blonde head as though trying to banish such an emotional storm, but she knew quite frighteningly she was desperate to go on seeking such intense physical pleasure. It was terrible, this uncontrollable desire, and her shimmering grey eyes were deeply expressive, so much so that Curt responded this time with a little force, more driving urgency, kissing her so deeply she lay quietly against him, deliberately choosing to relinquish her heart.

'Don't do this if you don't mean it,' she begged.

'And I don't?' His low murmur was lost against

her throat. 'Oh, Katy, you're necessary, but not these damned buttons.'

Conditioning overrode her own feelings. Her slender fingers locked and entwined with his own hand. 'Curt?'

'Far enough,' he said mockingly, unaware that his clear green eyes were almost dark. 'Lately, Katy ...' he began.

'Lately, what?'

Whatever he might have answered she was not to hear. Jo-Ann's piercingly loud call sounded down the hall, at such a frequency Katharine felt her own ears vibrating.

'Curt, darling!'

'I see no reason why she should spend her first night alone,' said Katharine coldly.

'What on earth are you talking about?' He very nearly hurt her, his winged brows drawing together.

'Jo-Ann. She loves you.'

'Rubbish!'

'You're not being helpful. I thought we were waiting for an early announcement.'

'Don't be unhappy!'

The soft caress in his voice had her shaking her head helplessly. She turned back to the piano, her hands trembling, astounded how much and how deeply she felt for him. Her grey eyes were emotion-laden, but she tilted her chin, trying to breathe normally. In a moment Jo-Ann would be upon them. 'Do I look all right?' Katharine asked.

'You've no idea!'

'Please!' she begged.

'You're beautiful, Katy, a little heart-torn at the moment. Keep those luminous eyes down. Jo-Ann's alarmingly shrewd.'

'And you have to fool her?'

'Little idiot!'

'Sweet talk, Curt Dangerfield. You're good at it. Even Sally knows that!'

'I'm serious. Really, Katy.' His gaze was still dark jade, lit now by a devastating humour.

'Take your kisses where you can,' she accused him.

'Especially with you. Play something, for God's sake. You looked terribly chaste at dinner, but now you're something else again. Jo-Ann doesn't miss a thing.'

'I don't particularly care. Maybe she'll realise you're no jewel of perfection.'

He smiled at her, his eyes glittering with sardonic amusement and much as he might try to deny it, a thwarted male passion. 'Smile, then.'

'No trick at all!'

When Jo-Ann, closely followed by Rada, finally burst into the drawing room Katharine was calmly discussing Sally's progress as a music student. Vehemently Rada broke in:

'For God's sake, is this where you are?'

'In my own drawing room.'

It took a moment for Rada to ingest the fact that she had better say no more, to her cousin at any rate. He could never be snarled at as she had constantly snarled at Jeff. In fact a look of dark hauteur had come on him.

'Katharine's just telling me she thinks Sally has real talent,' he told her.

'Doesn't that make you happy, dear?' Jo-Ann asked gaily.

'I'd rather she had some looks to speak of,' Rada replied rudely.

'You weren't all that good-looking yourself ten years ago,' Jo-Ann said sweetly. 'You've improved!'

'And everyone knows you're thirty.'

'A dirty word. Naturally I never discuss my age, but surely you're more?'

'Make a clean break, ladies,' Curt said rather tersely. 'Katharine, don't let us keep you. You said you were rather tired.'

'She looks absolutely wide-eyed to me,' Jo-Ann said searchingly.

'Sheer bravado. Run along,' Curt ordered indulgently as if to a child. 'A game of bridge, Jo-Ann. It seems like a sober game. I'm sure Rada and Martha will join us.'

'How depressing!' Jo-Ann collapsed into a chair.

'It doesn't make any difference to me,' Rada said on purpose. That way they would all stay together.

'Let's go for a ride. A bit of looniness,' Jo-Ann suggested, and Katharine waited to hear no more of it. She knew for a fact that Jo-Ann meant it and Rada would prove no competitor, for Rada couldn't ride at all. Incredibly she was nervous of horses. Katharine opened the double cedar door and walked out, moving fast. Ten minutes later she heard voices in the courtyard and Jo-Ann's laugh, simply oozing seduction, floating along the veranda and in the French doors. So they were going on that idiotic ride. A huge moon, the music of the cicadas, the swish of the thick grass on the savannahs. She couldn't think too badly of Jo-Ann, for she liked her. *Curt* ... well, Curt with his talent should be famous.

CHAPTER SIX

IT took Katharine a long time to realise she was being followed. The chestnut gelding she was riding had plenty of life in him, but she swung him about, holding him easily. A coloured stockman on an old work horse broke cover of the bush, making directly for her. She sat her horse, staring at the approaching figure, failing to recognise him until he was a few yards away. He was old, his dark glowing face seamed with grey. She looked at him without surprise. Neither of them smiled, but both knew what he had come for.

'How are you, Barney?'

'No complaints, miss.' He had swung along beside her, looking at her almost with pity. 'The Boss don't know I'm here, yet. I've come from Arrow Head—took me all yesterday. I camped out overnight.'

'You've something to tell me?'

'I have, miss.'

'About Darin?'

'Yes. Don't be afraid, miss, he's all right.'

'Where is he?' she asked breathlessly.

'Not far from here.' Barney waved a noncommittal hand about. 'He's pretty sick—picked up a fever. I've done the best I can.'

Katharine's voice was brittle with strain. 'But why are you helping him, Barney?'

'I owe him,' Barney said simply. 'Never treated me like a black.'

'You could get into trouble with Mr Dangerfield.'

'I know that,' Barney said, and swallowed. 'No need to get upset. Little chance of puttin' anything over the Boss. I owe this to Darin before I let on to the Boss. That's if he don't know already.'

'What's the message?' she asked.

'No message, miss. Your brother knows where you is. He hasn't asked for you, but I reckon he needs help. The Boss never sacked him—he just made off. I reckon he knows somethin' about the cattle, maybe not. I know nothin' myself and I've been on Half-Moon all me life. Easy enough to steal cattle on a property this size. Some organised gang, maybe from the South. We can't cover everywhere. Someone has been givin' out information, someone knows where the herds are runnin'—that kind of thing.'

And not beyond Darin, Katharine thought, her soft mouth twisting. 'How ill is he?' she asked.

'Pretty sick.'

'Where has he been all this time?'

'Dunno. Easy in this kinda country.'

'I'll come with you.'

'More better you tell the Boss.'

'No.' Katharine shook her blonde head. 'No one can prove anything against Darin. I have to see him first.'

'All right!' Barney nodded his old head gravely,

'but there's only one way you're gonna do it and that's tell lies to the Boss. Wouldn't do it myself!'

'You found him, Barney, didn't you? You're a very good tracker. You were behind me for almost an hour.'

'Darin needed a shelter,' Barney said doggedly. 'He can't run no longer. This is a secret, miss, between you and me, for a little while, anyway. You get a chance to talk sense to your brother. You can trust me, missy.'

'I know that.'

'I can't bring him here,' Barney cautioned. 'Too close to the Big House.'

'We'll ride,' Katharine decided.

'Kinda rough,' Barney objected.

'Don't worry about that, I'll make out. How will I find you? I'll have to go back to the house. Think up some excuse.'

'I'll hang about here. Don't worry, no one seen me. I can hide out most anyplace, better 'an Darin.'

'We'll have to leave soon!' Katharine said, looking worried.

'He ain't dyin',' Barney said almost cheerfully. 'Just sick.'

'I don't want him sick.'

'Tell the Boss, then. Your choice, missy. I'll go along with you.'

'I want to see my brother first,' she insisted. 'I want to hear his story from his own mouth. He must be pretty desperate.'

'Funny,' Barney observed in his soft melodious

voice, 'he doesn't seem to care much!'

Katharine sat lost in amazement. 'Just give me the chance to see him, then we'll go straight to Mr Dangerfield.'

'That's what I'm here for.'

'Then we won't waste any more time. I'll concoct some story and be back as soon as I can. Does Darin need food?'

'Got some.' Barney grinned for the first time, displaying excellent strong white teeth.

'All right.'

'It might be pretty hard going, missy,' he warned.

'You don't have to worry, Barney. We'll get there!'

All the way back to the homestead, Katharine's heart raced painfully. Darin meant so much to her. He was *her* worry. She knew in her bones she should tell Curt, but that might drive Darin away. Darin trusted her. She began to realise that there was no clear road to anything. For another reason she had to see Darin first: she had to find out what Rada meant to him. Rada, like some exotic dark snake in their midst. Rada cared less than nothing for Darin. Little flurries of dust whipped up about the gelding's flying hooves. It was intensely hot, not a cloud in the peacock sky. The leaves of the trees were sparkling, quartz green, edge on to the sun. A goanna raced out of the bush and saw her, raced up a tree and clung there for dear life, its forked tongue flicking.

If Darin had a fever, was he lucid? In the face of his illness, it was irresponsible to continue to hide him. He had enough problems without this further complication. The knowledge that she should go straight to Curt, if necessary beg for her brother, warred with Katharine's decision. It was simply that she was filled with an immeasurable pity for her brother. Was that so bad? She was, she realised, as she raced through the huge wrought iron gates of the homestead, quite frightened of Curt. He would make a formidable enemy, not a man to be treated lightly or fooled. She cantered into the yards and a coloured boy in a vivid red work shirt took charge of the gelding, leaving her free to hurry back to the house. Her skin was overheated, and her silvery grey eyes were oddly brilliant. Even the flowers and shrubs of the garden were almost overpowering her with their sweet, heavy fragrance.

'Got a minute?' She was scarcely inside the cool glittering interior when Curt grasped her arm. He pulled her closer, staring down into her upturned, flushed face—an interminable scrutiny. 'Where have you been?' he demanded tersely.

'Oh, out and about, seeing as much as I can of the station.'

'You don't have to see it in one morning. You look feverish.'

'Don't fuss!'

His hand tightened. 'Don't chat *me* up, Katy!'

'I'm sorry, I didn't mean to.'

'You could try telling me what's really on your mind.'

'Why, nothing!' She looked up at him innocently, then quickly away again, jarred by his turbulent expression.

'Casual words, lady, when you look anything but. Naturally I won't inquire further. It might put you even more on the defensive.'

'There's nothing wrong,' she said, her cheeks burning. 'Please, Curt, you're hurting me!'

'I'd like to keep on, and I would, only you look so damned defenceless. Don't say nothing's wrong when there's a lot of things that aren't right.' His normally dark velvet voice was almost metallic. 'Why can't you trust me, Katy? Why? You must know I'll always help you.'

'There's simply nothing to tell you,' she said, trying in vain to pull away from him. 'I went for a ride, I got overheated. That's it!'

'All right!' he burst out contemptuously, his chiselled mouth set. 'You sure love to follow a tortuous path. By the way, we're taking a trip over to Kurabee this afternoon—the Boynes' place. They're our neighbours on the south-western border. Want to come? Jo-Ann went to school with the girls.'

'Thank you, no,' she said tautly. 'I'd only be in the way.'

'What if I said I *want* you to come? It's supposed to be a pleasure trip!'

'You give the orders,' she said almost bitterly.

A sudden spurt of anger shook him. He grasped

her by the shoulders, his strong fingers biting into her collarbones. 'I thought I was being pretty kind to you.'

'You'll all have lots to catch up on,' she protested, the tears very nearly coming to her eyes and further angering him. 'I'm the outsider. I'll be perfectly all right here.'

'True,' he said with unbearable irony. 'You're safer on Half-Moon than you'll ever be anywhere else.'

'When are you leaving?' She could feel herself trembling under his hands as he surely must.

'Actually we were waiting for you.'

'And now?' She kept her eyes lowered, her heavy lashes down.

'In less than an hour,' he said briefly. 'It's only a flip in a plane. Are you sure you're decided?'

'Is Sally going?' She had no choice but to throw in a red herring.

'Certainly,' he said dryly. 'I wouldn't leave her behind, as you very well know.'

Katharine tried to smile at him, which was difficult, because he looked as if he could choke her. 'It's a beautiful day. I might go for a swim, maybe another ride. I'm very fortunate to be in such a lovely place.'

'Have it your own way!' he said just as tersely as he could.

'It's never my intention to make you angry!' She put out a hand helplessly, but he ignored it.

'You say one thing, Katharine, but you mean

different. Don't think I'll drown in your silver eyes
—I won't. There are degrees of anger. I'm not all
that angry at the moment, otherwise you'd know.
Do what you think best, but take care. Stick to the
beaten tracks. I've grown quite used to you.'

'But you still don't approve?'

'No.' His green eyes were narrowed, faintly hostile. 'You're a deep one, Katharine Sutton. Now I'm
in a hurry. You know how it is?'

'Yes, and I don't feel too badly. Jo-Ann is very
attractive. Congratulations!'

'She's truthful too. Lies are always a mistake!'

There was an awful challenging directness to his
gaze. She couldn't sustain it. 'May I go now?' she
asked.

'Please do,' he said very politely, utterly remote
now, walking away from her back through the west
wing of the house.

She put up a shaky hand to brush back her silky
fall of hair. The wind had skeined it all about her
flushed face. She felt on the brink of disaster.

Apart from the birds that reigned supreme everywhere, the only life they spotted on the whole ride
was a young bull coming down on the creek to drink.
It planted its forehooves, sniffed the clear water,
then elegantly bent its glistening neck. It was obvious that Barney wanted to return it to the herd,
but he continued to ride up ahead of Katharine,
machete in hand, making the path easier for her to
negotiate. Almost tremblingly she noticed a huge

amethyst snake uncoil its long length in front of her before it slithered swiftly away along a branch. She rode under it with her nape crawling, fully expecting a thick slimy body to fall heavily on her shoulder.

Several times along the way Barney looked behind him, grunting to himself. Katharine was almost tempted to scream as well. This was very nearly jungle, alive with snakes. It would be just her luck to encounter a taipan. Just thinking about it could make one go into hysterics, but she had to keep her head. Barney was a good guide. He was more at home in the wild bush than she was in a safe bed. She, too, had the queer feeling that something was stalking them with relentless perfection and her head was constantly tilted in an attitude of listening.

Somewhere in this green tangled fastness was Darin. No wonder no one could find him! It would be an almost impossible task. Another upward glance and she saw a peculiarly marked snake pressed close to the long shaft of a tree. She put her tongue to her dry mouth, swinging round as a brilliant blue and yellow parrot let out an aggressive, warning shriek. Under the steaming belt of the trees there was hardly any sunlight, but had she eyes for it, it was fascinating. At their approach, the birds began to rise up all around them, every colour of the rainbow, their voices unbelievably loud. The thick springy grass and the canopy of trees was jade green, the trees flowering in a profusion of pink and coral and an electric violet. Such a beautiful, bewildering variety of them!

A small spotted tree goanna, yellow and grey, left off robbing a bird's nest to mark their progress, and Katharine knew this kind of country would come alive at night with animal life. At the edge of the rose gums there rose up a low granite wall, masked with thick vegetation, and a great staghorn that grew on the bark of a giant eucalypt. Barney looked behind him and held up the pinkish palm of his hand, to halt her.

'We're here, missy.'

She dismounted at once, handing the reins to Barney and rushing to she didn't know where.

'Wait, miss. You won't find it.'

'Is it a cave?'

Barney made sure of the horses then came towards her. 'Easy, miss. You're safe. The snakes didn't get you.'

'There were quite a few about.'

Barney moved ahead of her, very nimbly for an old man, pulling away at a thick screen of tangled ferns and vines. They came away with great ease until Katharine realised they had been chopped away long hours before. Barney caught her frenzied sigh.

'Go in. This is your brother's hiding place.'

'Oh, Darin!' She no longer knew what to think. Her heart came into her throat as she bent her head, her eyes trying to pierce the sudden gloom. Outside Barney was hacking more vines away and the interior of the small cave lightened. An unguessed-at wave of pity came at her.

'Darin?'

She still couldn't see him, and a tremor of fear hit her. She had trusted Barney, followed him here without a word to anyone, no sense of caution. Could he have deceived her? Her voice bounced back softly from the walls of the cave. 'Darin?'

A moan answered her and she felt an uprush of shame. Barney had helped both of them. She stepped across the floor of the cave, feeling icy to her finger-tips. Darin was lying on some camping gear, his skin above the thick tawny stubble on his cheeks and chin a dreadful grey with mottled red patches. He could have been any age, not a young man. She dropped to her knees, weeping now as if she was in an awful nightmare. 'Darin! Is this how I find you?' Her tender hands ran over his heated face, the scorching brow. He was mumbling again, tossing his head fretfully to one side.

She stood up quickly, calling behind her: 'Barney!'

It was vital now to get him back to the homestead. No more secrets, no evasions. Something had to be done no matter the cost. Darin could die here. She could no longer wait to hear from his own mouth the story of his innocence or guilt. A shadow fell across the cave opening and if it was much too tall for Barney she didn't question it. She spoke shakily, the tears in her voice. 'Oh, Barney, he could die here!'

'He won't. He's too tough.'

Her heart contracted. She spun around, her hand going to her throat, utterly beaten. 'The hunter to the hunting ground!'

'Don't goad me a step further.'

'I've sentenced him, haven't I?' she cried wildly. 'I led you here.'

'Be quiet!' he said cruelly. 'Just be thankful I'm here.'

She watched him drop to his knees, leaning over her unconscious brother. He looked pitiless, indifferent, a strong, hard, handsome man. Dangerous to her, dangerous to Darin. Her voice cracked. 'Don't hurt him. If he's done wrong, he's been punished!' Her whisper was desperate, barely audible. She came close to him. '*Please*, Curt!'

'What do you think I am, some kind of monster?' He looked back at her as if he hated her and she ran her hands violently through her own hair, spilling it in silky disorder about her pale face. 'I don't want him to be punished any more.' She put her hand on his arm, feeling the iron tension in him.

'I asked you a question. What would you do for your brother? Stay with me on Half-Moon?'

'Yes, anything!'

'Then it's done. I'll take care of him.'

'What is it? What is it you want?' she demanded.

'You,' he said coldly, his dark face quite ruthless, his cleft chin pronounced.

'Then I'll make you a solemn promise!' A tear slid down her cheek and fell on his hand. He brushed it off angrily and lifted Darin in his arms.

'I could beat you! I will, when I get the chance. Barney?' He lifted his voice explosively and the old aboriginal stockman jumped to attention, certain he would have done better to go to the Boss in the first place.

'Yes, Boss?'

'Before I murder you, ride back to the homestead. Give Martha all the details, and get her to fly in Doctor Briant. He's more discreet than most. Then get Viv to bring the jeep to the edge of the clearing, as far in as he can.'

'I knew you was behind us,' shrugged Barney.

'Did you really think you could pull it off?'

'I used to be good. Remember?'

'You're getting old. You're slipping.'

'Taught you a thing or two,' Barney said, greatly daring.

'So you did—the only thing that's saving you. Now get going!'

'Need a hand with Darin?'

'I'll get him up on my horse. I'll lead him in.'

'What about Missy? Will I take her?' asked the old man.

'Missy can damned well walk!'

'It's pretty rough . . .'

'Say another word, Barney, and I swear . . . !'

'I'm going, Boss,' Barney said with alacrity and a soft pitying glance for Katharine, who had not come into the conversation at all. She looked as delicate as a lily or a moving bird on the wing, but the Boss was bent on punishing her. Women needed to feel the sting of anger. Barney wheeled his horse around and headed it for the homestead. He was sorry to leave Missy, but there was nothing else for it. Defying the Boss would lead him exactly nowhere, except maybe damnation!

Katharine couldn't sleep. She lay in the huge four-poster bed going over and over the events of the afternoon. She shivered remembering, but at least Darin was safe. That was all she *had* to remember. Whatever Darin had done, Curt had promised to protect him. His reason she couldn't search for; she had sold her soul for it. She turned her face into the cool nest of pillows, her whole body blazing. How could so much tenderness and cruelty go into the one man? Darin was a part of her, her brother. Surely Curt could accept that? Darin was weak, unreliable, the picture wasn't pretty, but their mother had always called him her golden boy. He had been that for both of them. The golden boy. She felt genuinely bereft that she could no longer feel proud of him. Still, she was filled with compassion—it was her nature. What she felt for Curt was deeper, stronger, a kind of agony that wrenched at her.

He had been in a wonderful rage; a thunderous silence that lasted all the way back to the house. Nothing could quench his thirst for hurting her and he wasn't finished with her yet. It would be impossible to make peace with him, but she had given her solemn promise to remain on Half-Moon. It was nerve-racking, an intolerable situation. He would have to release her from her promise.

Footsteps came to her door and she sat up in perplexity. The door opened and a torch light flashed over her. 'Katharine?' The tone was firm, not concerned about waking her.

'I'm awake!' She leaned over and turned on the lamp on the small table beside her, half in, half out of the lake of light. She looked very fragile, her hair cascading over her bare shoulders, a delicately endangered silver-blonde in the huge mahogany bed. Her eyes were apprehensive, half dazed. Curt stood in the doorway watching her, no trace of friendliness or serenity in his dark face. He was still dressed in the same clothes he had been wearing all day, so he hadn't gone to bed. His eyes slipped over her, poised so warily, and she leaned a little forward so that her face and hair fell into the rosy gold pool of light. 'What is it?'

He seemed to relax a little. 'I haven't come to claim any non-existent rights,' he said with hard mockery. 'Your brother has regained consciousness.'

'Can't you say Darin?'

'No, I can't.' He spoke with a take-it-or-leave-it arrogance. 'You want everything, Katharine, but everything you can't have. Get up. This kind of thing gets us nowhere. I'm acting pretty well in the circumstances.'

'Shall I dress?' she queried.

'Haven't you a robe or something?'

Hurriedly she murmured: 'Of course!' But not the charming little froth that lay over the end of a chair. She was too fully aware of his eyes on her, astonishingly brilliant. He was insensitive to her dilemma, so she slipped swiftly out of the bed, crossed to the mirrored wardrobe and took out a loose flowered patio dress in a sky blue and gold. Determinedly she pulled it over her head, grateful for its silky envelopment.

'A child again!' he said after a brief glance at her. 'Come along, Katharine, comfort your brother. It's all you've ever wanted.'

They were facing each other now and she had never been more conscious of his height, his lean-ness, his breadth of shoulder. He looked immensely strong and vital, his shirt collar carelessly ruffled. It wasn't simply that she was without shoes that made her feel so agonisingly ineffectual. She was the foolish, untutored child he evidently saw her as. He was standing quite still, a curious trick of his, for he was neither cool nor detached.

She said in a low voice with pain in it. 'I never wanted to involve you in my problems, Curt.'

'That's no use to me now. I'm up to my neck.' The light caught the icy sheen of his eyes.

'Haven't you one kind word for me?'

'Sure, you're beautiful, but I'm curious to know what goes on inside you.'

'The usual things, I care about people!'

Her slightness and smallness was too much to be borne. His dark face grew sombre, not in the least inclined to smile. It was, as she had realised from the beginning, a demanding kind of face, the face of a man of considerable pride and achievement. She had seen him with a dozen moods on him, but now he looked unbearably cynical, self-ironic. It hurt her. He took her arm and she shivered. 'Are you coming or not?' he asked very crisply indeed. 'You look as though you need a helping hand. Come along, Katharine, a cosy little chat with your brother, but remember you're not completely free to do as you like!'

She glanced at him quickly and her glance wavered. She felt a sudden upthrust of inevitable excitement. His hand on her forearm was hard and possessive. He had exhausted his supply of indulgence.

'Try to understand,' she said pleadingly, her skin under his hand tightening electrically.

'Believe me, I'm trying!' Almost compulsively his thumb had fallen to caressing her wrist, his hold on her compelling and achieved very easily, yet anger touched his face. It was tormenting to have things so strained and untrusting between them. Once he had held her in his arms, full of an undeniable passion, now he was a hair-trigger away from hurting her. Such a puzzle! Even the nearness of him, angry as he was, was exquisite. She never wanted to break free of him no matter what the cost. He wasn't a man to forget and no woman could tame him. She looked up at him swiftly with all her small torments there in her face.

'One more thing—I know you'll never believe me, but I love you!'

The change in him was stunning. It was like throwing an electric switch. 'You've no idea what you've just said!'

Her heart shrank and she almost recoiled from him. 'I told you you wouldn't believe me.'

'Convince me. No fuss.' He sounded hard and businesslike, anything but lover-like, a glittery look on him. He dragged her ruthlessly back into an alcove, almost lifting her off the ground. 'Do you say this kind of thing often?' His hands and his voice communicated a swift urgency. 'Tell me!'

'Never!'

'Then why don't you damned well trust me? Isn't that an important part of it? Loving? Oh, never mind. I've nothing left in restraint. I'll shape you my way—God knows you're young enough!'

Katharine turned her mouth up just to please him and he claimed it with such passionate fury she was stilled into a near-oblivion, her senses swimming, no area of resistance in her soft, yielding body. It was impossible to match the devouring desire she had aroused in him. Such a blinding rush of headlong emotion left her quivering and spent. He was capable of anything. She just wanted to go on giving and giving—anything to please and placate him. Her heart was beating too rapidly. He lifted his head briefly and drew an audible breath.

'I'm hurting you.'

'Impossible!' she whispered.

'I am. There's so little of you I could crush you!'

She looked so very young and vulnerable, her heart in her cloud-soft grey eyes, instinctively he lowered his head again, kissing her this time with control on himself, such a devastating tenderness, an underlying need now to arouse her as she had aroused him, that she felt herself melting; her head twisted back into the curve of his shoulder, responding convulsively. All the towering protective walls she had built round herself were crumbling. He was stripping them all away from her. He knew her better than she knew herself. He knew everything there was to know about making love to her. She didn't know she was making small, yearning sounds against his mouth.

He let go of her suddenly, holding her steady. 'I've meant to do that about a dozen times in the past few hours,' he muttered.

'But you seemed so remote and indifferent!'

'Maybe. All I know is I'd better let go of you. See your brother alone. I'll wait for you in the study.'

The change in Darin was extraordinary. He almost looked jaunty. Washed, clean-shaven, the good bones of his face very pronounced, the bright patches of colour fading, he measured Katharine's advance as though he was never more surprised to see anyone.

'I didn't bargain on your interfering in this, Katlin.'

'Don't be a fool, Darin. You're my brother. I

didn't want anyone or anything to threaten you. How are you?' She crossed to the bed and looked down at him.

'Much better. Loaded with antibiotics. It's a bad business, I can tell you.'

'What happened? You must tell me.'

'It's a long story—too long. Pull up a chair.'

'I know about Rada, if that's what you mean.' Looking carefully behind her, Katharine sank into a small curve-backed chair. 'You gave her the gold collar.'

For an instant the hazel eyes blazed. 'How do you know that?'

'She was wearing it the very first night I came here.'

'How incredibly stupid! I can't accept that of Rada!'

'Women are vain. You had no right to that necklace.'

'Forget that!' Darin said wearily. 'You got the house, didn't you? Wasn't it enough?'

'You could have had all of it,' she pointed out. 'You chose to leave us. How did it start, the smuggling, the rest of it? I have a right to know.'

'You're not my keeper,' he grumbled. 'You sound like Mum. She stifled me. She did a good job on you too. You don't know what it's like, Kat, having no money, and seeing it all around you. Power, the big time. Say a thing and everyone moves on the double. No need to prove anything, you just are. Curt's got it made!'

'And you chose to cheat him. The man who had befriended you and offered you the chance of managing a station.'

'Not good enough, Kat. I'm a man on the make, always have been. That's what you don't understand.'

'I understand you could go to jail.'

'I don't think so!' In a rough brotherly way he slapped at her hand. 'I'm not the only member of this exclusive circle involved.'

'Who then—Rada?'

'A woman's intuition. What a gift! I thought of it, Rada put it into operation. At first it was just a crazy way we had of talking, day dream value to fill in the conversation, but Rada figured it out. She had the contacts. I was in it that one time. Just a hit and run job, and after that I wanted out. Rada and her friends got the bulk of the loot anyway. The trouble was Rada could put the finger on me at any time. She loves her profits. In fact, she's no good. You could even say she's a bit mad!'

'She doesn't care a jot about you.'

'Does it matter?' he replied bitterly. 'I believed her for a while. She was going to come away with me. I was crazy about her—Rada, and no one else. It was only that one time with me. I intended to stay out after that.'

'You mean you were ready to commit every sin for her.'

'And then some! You have to admit she's got something.' He glanced at Katharine curiously as though he found her moralising hard to understand. 'Oh, grow up, Katlin. Curt's a millionaire. What's a few hundred head matter?'

'That's hardly the point!'

He couldn't evade her searching glance. 'I know. I'm sorry, Kat, damned sorry—on lots of counts. Curt was pretty good to me. I've got the greatest respect for him.'

'But you didn't mind stealing his cattle.'

'He's got enough, more than he could ever want. Still, I'm sorry now. Anyway, I took time out to check Rada's connections—an exercise in futility. Curt had already caught up with them. He evened up the score and then plenty.'

'And Rada?'

'He was on to her, of course. He even set her up. Her pals sold her out pretty smart. No one likes prison and they were given an out. There was an almighty scene—didn't you hear it?'

'I heard nothing.'

'You wouldn't in a house this size, I suppose.'

'When did you regain consciousness?' she asked then.

'About two hours ago. Curt wasn't very agreeable. I've had quite a shake-down. He's got Rada over a barrel. He's a very shrewd operator, our Curt. I should have had him as a partner. Rada loses the kid.'

'Sally?' Katharine was taken aback.

'Curt becomes her joint guardian with old Mrs Lewis. Sally will probably live with her grandmother. She's a nice little kid. I can't imagine how Rada had her. Don't worry, Rada's not too sour on the deal. She'll get plenty to shove off and it's better than going to jail. Curt just has to say the word. She was pretty steamed up at first—frantically denied everything, tore into me, the incompetent bungler, then when she realised he was on to her she just went to pieces. The whole collapse lasted about a half hour, then she got her second wind. Rada knows exactly what she wants.'

'Well, she's not getting it!' Katharine pointed out dryly. 'Don't sound as if you admire her. She would have left you to die!'

'I figured that out all by myself. It's all right, I'm a big boy now, just a bit rusty at the moment. When I think of the time I wasted trying to pin the swag on Rada and Curt knew all the time. I could have saved myself a lot of pain.'

'You deserved it.'

'I needed the cash!' he said bluntly. 'There was a time when Rada looked and sounded pretty different to me. It was quite a shock to find out just how mean she really is. I'm a bad judge of women. Once she was eager, hooking into me, promising me the world. She found the right people for the job— not professionals she couldn't control but people who could handle themselves. Curt has done business with them anyway. They're all paid up now and happy to get out of it so lightly with only a huge belt in the pocket. They'll never come into it again. He has complete control of everything.'

'What about you?' She looked at him with un-expected censure.

'I'm finished here by any standards. Sold up. In fact I'm out on the morrow. The big man doesn't want me here, contaminating the homestead. I'm being shifted to Base Hospital for a few days. After that, I might take in New Zealand. It's a beautiful country, I hear. You know, Kat,' he went on, 'there's an odd factor in all this. It's not Rada, nor the child, and Curt wouldn't give a damn if I rotted in hell. There's a chink in his armour. I can't believe it, but it's got to be. Why else would he have arranged it this way? No one gets hurt except the boys on the Coast, and then only in the pocket.'

Katharine sat quite still hesitating for a moment, then she said: 'From his conversations with me, Darin, Curt wants to protect Sally. Rada isn't good for her own child. Worse, she doesn't even care for her.'

'That could be,' said Darin, sounding uncon-vinced.

'That's it.'

'Maybe. It's been a long day.'

'You're tired.' She put her hand on his arm and pressed it.

'Played out, girl. Make no mistake about it, I was double-crossed.'

'It seems to me, Darin, you're mostly to blame. Rada just happened to be around at a critical moment.'

'It could never have happened without Rada.

She was the serpent. She was going to come away with me—she promised. We couldn't do it without money. What other way was there to make some ready cash?'

'Work for it.'

'Don't be so damn virtuous! Properly handled we could have pulled it off.'

'I don't agree. You're a dimwit beside Curt.'

'It was Rada who derailed the situation. She got greedy. Don't worry, kid, I'll get myself a new face. I'll still land myself a first-class job.'

'Not in this State you won't!' she said almost sadly.

'Or the next or the next. The Dangerfields, dear, run an empire. I just wanted a piece of the action.'

'Incredible!' Katharine sighed, almost at a loss for words. 'How could you imagine you were entitled to any part of it?'

'It wasn't only me,' Darin defended himself. 'Rada thought she was entitled to a fair share as well. Jeff was Curt's cousin.'

'Good God, Darin, plenty of people have rich relations without dreaming of touching a penny of it. You'd better start seeing things straight. You wouldn't want this kind of thing to finish up a ritual?'

'I've learnt my lesson,' Darin said, after a little. 'This fever alone nearly killed me.'

'You were in no real danger. You'd have come out of it even in the cave with only Barney to look after you.'

'I never said anything to Barney,' Darin considered. 'Thank him.'

'I already have. Remember when we were children?' she said painfully.

'That was an age ago.'

'I loved you then, looked up to you. Mother used to call you her golden boy. She always cared more for you than me.'

'Then she was stupid.'

'In that way, perhaps. You're not really that admirable, though it breaks my heart to say so.'

'I'll make it. Listen, Kat, I haven't sunk too low. I lost my head over a woman. It happens all the time. Nearly everyone has at least one disaster. Maybe if I'd met a nice girl, someone like you, things would have been different.'

'You may yet meet her,' Katharine promised. 'I'll pray for you.'

'Good girl! You've always been that—very loyal. Yes, I remember you, Kat. Silver plaits and big eyes. You were the prettiest little girl in the world. Come to that, you're still the tops.'

Katharine leaned forward and kissed his lean cheek. 'Please learn something from all this, Darin. Don't ever get caught again.'

Darin chortled somewhat reluctantly. 'I know what you mean. I won't. There could be only one Rada in a man's life.'

'The wicked charmer. Just as well!'

'I've come to my senses, Kat. I'm not the sentimental type. No more complications.' He turned

185

and smiled at her and it took her back all the years. She was the sentimental one. 'Turn out the light, Sis, right at this moment I want to go to sleep.'

She got up obligingly, walking to the door and switching off the main light. 'Goodnight, Darin. God bless. See you in the morning.'

'Thank you, little sister. And listen, Rada was raving on about you and Curt. She seemed pretty sure of her facts. Livid, if you ask me. She hadn't a hope in hell there and many's the time I told her. If you can land him, hang on like hell. He's nothing less than a superman. Even without all the dough he'd still zoom ahead.'

'I know.' Her slight frame was etched in the doorway against the hall light.

'You either have it or you don't,' Darin agreed wryly. 'Goodnight!'

'Believe me, Darin, you can make something of yourself. Start again!'

'What's my reason?'

'We've all got to go on improving ourselves.'

'Well, damn it, let's go!'

Katharine shut the door on him, smiling. Darin was an unabashed sinner, she couldn't pretend otherwise. All the events of the past weeks had fully illumined his character. He was lucky. He would be given another chance. She began to hurry along the hallway, sunk in her thoughts. Darin in a way was almost a total stranger to her. Life really was funny. For the first time in her life she could see her brother clearly. She reached the study and threw open the door, her expression alive, almost passionate.

'You waited!' she exclaimed.

'I said I would.' He stood up and walked towards her. 'What is it now, give him another chance a thousand miles from here?'

She shook her head soundlessly, just staring up at him. Vivid energy and integrity and everything worthy. She loved him. 'Nothing like that,' she whispered at last.

'What, then?' He put out a hand and brushed back her hair. 'I'll tell you now, nothing doing. Darin has to work out his own salvation.'

'I agree.'

'You *agree*? Katharine, how extraordinary!'

'That's all I wanted you to know.'

'And I need no more encouragement. You promised me you'd stay with me.'

Her mouth parted, but no words came out, just a strange rising fever.

'I can see you don't understand me,' he said smoothly. 'Marry me, Katharine. Certainly there's not another woman in the world who's going to hear that offer.'

'*Marry* you?'

'That's the catch!'

She hit out at him in a nervous reaction and he caught her up easily. 'Life would be just too tame without you.'

'There would be no life without *you*. I've no choice!'

187

Her words hit him like arrows. 'You'll never get away from me!'

'Such a pity! I'd never want to.' She turned her face up to him, helpless with love. His fingers touched her creamy skin, threaded through the long silky strands of her hair.

'It was too late for me that very first day,' he said with a faint shade of mockery.

'I feel guilty. I very nearly hated you.'

'Why?' His brilliant green eyes demanded an answer.

'I don't know,' she said truthfully. 'You seemed to know too much about me. I never expected anyone so vivid, so challenging. I never expected a man who would love me. Not in a lifetime.'

'Life holds nothing but surprises, Katharine. I promised myself you from the very first moment. I knew then it wouldn't be the last time I'd find you asleep. You're very responsive awake!'

'You know you're very special!' Her words came out like a soft, yearning sigh. 'Kiss me, my dearest, undeniable tyrant, I can't seem to do without it!'

'As though I can! What I feel for you would take aeons to describe. Right now I'm pretty desperate— I hope you realise.'

She was trembling, but her young voice was ardent, filled with a wonderful elation, yet very serious. 'Feel my heart!' she begged him. 'Feel it beat for you. What more do you want?'

'Katharine——!' There was an odd break in his

voice. He swept her up easily, carrying her to the long sofa, kissing her until she could think no longer, nor wanted to. Love was the greatest necessity of all, and her love for Curt knew no bounds.

March Paperbacks

A LYON'S SHARE *by Janet Dailey*
Joan loved her boss, Brandt Lyon; but so, it seemed, did the delightful Angela!

LAIRD OF DOORN *by Sue Peters*
The friendship between Sue and Duncan was developing most satisfactorily. Then Fiona took a hand ...

THE SILVER LINK *by Mary Wibberley*
Sara hadn't expected her new boss to be the one man who could remind her of a past she wanted to forget.

DREAMTIME AT BIG SKY *by Dorothy Cork*
Jackson Brand had once pushed Reya out of his life. But now she was back ...

THE INTRUDER *by Jane Donnelly*
Richard Lingard threatened the happiness of Daisy's sister. Could she foil him?

SWANS' REACH *by Margaret Way*
Rachael would probably have hated anyone who bought her old home, Swans' Reach – but when it proved to be Dominic Retford ...

THE MARK OF TREGARRON *by Lucy Gillen*
Toni's Cornish holiday would have been perfectly peaceful, except for the disturbing Jake Tregarron!

INHERIT THE SUN *by Rebecca Stratton*
Would the glamour of the South Seas compensate Beth for her battle of wills with her arrogant cousin Louis?

ALIEN WIFE *by Anne Mather*
Abby's marriage to Luke was purely for motives of revenge – or was it?

THE VALLEY OF PALMS *by Jean S. MacLeod*
Why did Elizabeth have to fall in love with Michael, when there was so much ill-feeling between their two families?

35p net

Available March 1977

Your Mills & Boon Selection

☐ 995
THE HOUSE OF STRANGE MUSIC
Margery Hilton

☐ 1056
WANDALILLI PRINCESS
Dorothy Cork

☐ 1060
THAT MAN BRYCE
Mary Wibberley

☐ 1063
THE GIRL AT DANES' DYKE
Margaret Rome

☐ 1070
DEAR INTRUDER
Jane Arbor

☐ 1073
COBWEB MORNING
Betty Neels

☐ 1079
THE HUNGRY TIDE
Lucy Gillen

☐ 1081
THE GARDEN OF DREAMS
Sara Craven

☐ 1084
ROSS OF SILVER RIDGE
Gwen Westwood

☐ 1089
STAR CREEK
Pamela Kent

☐ 1091
THE SWEET SURRENDER
Rose Burghley

☐ 1094
VALLEY OF PARADISE
Margaret Rome

☐ 1099
AUTUMN TWILIGHT
Anne Hampson

☐ 1102
THE SUN OF SUMMER
Lilian Peake

☐ 1113
A LESSON IN LOVING
Margaret Way

☐ 1124
EAST TO BARRYVALE
Yvonne Whittal

☐ 1127
DEAR SIR
Mary Burchell

☐ 1130
THE CHILD OF JUDAS
Violet Winspear

☐ 1134
THE DANCE OF COURTSHIP
Flora Kidd

☐ 1139
DARK PURSUER
Jane Donnelly

☐ 1143
SUNSET CLOUD
Anne Hampson

☐ 1154
DEAR BENEFACTOR
Anne Hampson

☐ 1157
ADAM'S RIB
Margaret Rome

☐ 1162
FORBIDDEN
Anne Mather

☐ 1169
CHATEAU D'ARMOR
Rebecca Stratton

☐ 1175
CALL OF THE OUTBACK
Anne Hampson

☐ 1187
CUPBOARD LOVE
Roberta Leigh

☐ 1193
TWO LOVES HAVE I
Mary Burchell

All priced at 30p each. Please tick your requirements and use
the handy order form overleaf.